The Dragons of Incendium

WYVERN'S PRINCE

DEBORAH COOKE

AUTHOR OF *WYVERN'S MATE*

ISBN: 978-1-927477-96-0

Prologue

The royal apartments in the palace of Incendium

I could MindBend Gemma," Troy offered.

"You could, but I prefer you tanned and not toasted," Drakina replied.

Gemma leaned against the wall of the corridor outside the new couple's chambers and eavesdropped on their conversation. She had intended to make one last visit to her new nephew before her own wedding and Drakina and Troy's subsequent departure for Terra, but hearing her name had brought her to a stop. She was glad of her keen dragon hearing, and her ability to remain completely still. An observer might have thought her struck to stone.

Fortunately, the serving maid who had left the chamber and failed to completely close the door was walking in the opposite direction. She hadn't noticed Gemma at all.

Felice, Gemma's pet pavofel, sat between Gemma's feet and the wall, then wrapped her tail around herself. The pavofel was a feline creature, bred to splendor on Cumae, with blue and green fur that resembled the feathers of the peacock known on other worlds. Felice was particularly pretty, sporting two dozen 'eyes' in the fur of her wide and lush tail. It always amazed Gemma how Felice could seem to disappear in the shadows, given the bright hues of her fur. Once seated, Felice was completely motionless. Only the glow of her luminous green eyes revealed her presence.

It must be true that pavofels chose their companions and caregivers, because Gemma and Felice seemed to understand each other perfectly.

"But you can't let her just marry Urbanus," Troy protested. "We know too much about his nature."

"I doubt we can stop her," Drakina replied, her tone suspiciously temperate. "Gemma is determined to marry Urbanus, just as Father planned, and ensure the treaty is made between the two kingdoms. You'll never change the thinking of two royal dragons."

"And you're not going to intervene?" Troy demanded. "Even if she's stepping into a trap?"

"You do not know that."

Troy snorted. "I don't have to be a MindBender to know that Urbanus is a sneak."

Drakina's tone turned thoughtful. "It *is* for the good of both kingdoms to make the alliance. Gemma knows as much as we do and she's agreed to marry him."

"But Urbanus arranged for the death of Arista..."

"Gemma knows that. Arista was her best friend."

"I know she knows that. It's why she hates me." Troy could be heard pacing. Gemma's heart filled with disgust that her older sister's husband had been the assassin who'd killed her best friend. Her argument, though, was with the instigator of the agreement, not the man who'd been given the job.

She knew enough about the Gloria Furora to understand that any choice Troy had been given wouldn't really have been a choice. His own death would probably have been the only other option available.

She might not be able to blame him for what he'd done, but she didn't have to like him.

How *could* Drakina have married a man, even her HeartKeeper, who could influence her thoughts? It was incomprehensible that Drakina was happy with a MindBender.

Maybe her big sister was more influenced by her husband than she realized.

"You should let me MindBend her about that, at least," Troy said and Gemma bristled at the suggestion. "The way she looks at me makes me uneasy."

"If you used your MindBending abilities, she would do more than glare at you. You would not survive the day."

Gemma nodded agreement with that.

"But why is she going? Why did she agree?"

"Gemma must have her reasons."

"That's it, isn't it?" Troy said. "She plans to avenge Arista."

Gemma straightened, impressed that he was the only one on Incendium who seemed to have guessed her plan. Or at least said it aloud. It was possible her father knew.

"I do not know." Drakina's tone was so mild that Gemma wondered whether her sister had guessed as well.

"But she can do that without marrying him!" Troy insisted. "There's a piece of the puzzle missing. Drakina, I can find it."

"I learned early in this palace that whenever you have not been told some detail, it is because that information is not yours to know," Drakina replied curtly. "It is folly to provoke tempers in a household of dragons."

"But..."

"Do you not understand that they are all on guard because they know what you can do? If you MindBend any of them, when I have vowed that you would not, even I will not be able to save you. Troy! Do not attempt this thing."

"You promised them I wouldn't use my powers?"

Troy was clearly surprised.

"It was the only way to gain you access to my father's court. You are Terran, a race he cannot tolerate. You are a MindBender, a kind he finds despicable. Even being Carrier of the Seed and my HeartKeeper was not enough for my father to allow you to step over the threshold given those credentials."

"Go ahead. Build my ego a little more."

Gemma smiled.

"Troy! I love you. Is that not sufficient?"

Troy made an exasperated noise, evidence that Drakina's love *wasn't* enough. Gemma had always thought that the minstrels who insisted that love conquered all were taking a simplistic view. Here was proof. "I feel like my only value is as a stud."

Drakina laughed, and her voice turned sultry. "Is that so bad? Come to bed, stud, and I will remind you of the benefits."

"It's not funny, princess. I need to use my powers. I need to *do* something."

"And you will have plenty to do once we get to Terra. I have invited my father to come and hunt, and he will arrive within days of our return there. You will be more than busy ensuring that no Terran notices a dragon king in the vicinity." Drakina sighed. "He is not accustomed to keeping a low profile, after all."

"Thanks for the warning."

"Look at the upside. His visit might improve his view of Terrans."

Troy scoffed, revealing his view of that possibility. Gemma was inclined to agree with him. Their father, Ouros, was slow to abandon any conviction. "Now, what about Gemma?"

"She can defend herself."

"What kind of family is this?" Troy demanded. I thought you watched over each other!"

Gemma felt the air chill and could easily imagine the look her sister was giving her new husband. She was tempted to peek and see if he took a step back.

"We also support each other's choices," Drakina said. "But..."

"But nothing, Troy." Drakina finally lost patience and her voice rose. There were probably sparks flying from the ends of her hair. "Gemma has *chosen*. I do not understand her decision. I have tried to talk to her about it, but she is determined. She *must* have a reason. She *must* have a plan. She clearly is not going to share it, and she *would* share it if she needed help."

"She could be wrong."

"It is less probable statistically that Gemma is wrong than any of my other sisters."

Gemma smiled and nodded at that.

Drakina continued. "She did train with the Warrior Maidens of Cumae, you know."

"And Prince Urbanus is one sneaky bastard. How can your father let her marry him at all?"

"He had his doubts. Gemma volunteered to secure the alliance."

"Why? It's nuts, princess."

"Gemma is not crazy."

"So, that's it? You're just going to let her go and if she's wrong, well, you still have ten more sisters?"

"She is *not* wrong. Gemma is never wrong."

Gemma heard Troy pacing the room. "And you won't let me use my powers to find out her plan, even if it might save her," he said with exasperation. "What's the point of our being together if we aren't a team?"

"Some would say our son Gravitas was the point."

"Do you really love me, Drakina, or did you just want the Seed from me?"

Gemma winced and moved away, unwilling to hear the rest of their argument. Were all marriages compromises, even those between HeartKeepers? Was the promise of true love a lie? Gemma didn't want it to be. Or was Drakina's happiness compromised because Troy was a MindBender? Gemma wished she knew for sure. She wanted the kind of marriage her parents had, but didn't think she'd get it.

She might as well marry Urbanus, conceive his son, and then kill him for his crime.

There was a good precedent for that in the mating ritual of her cousins, after all. They always killed the Carrier of the Seed once his precious burden had been delivered. She could raise the boy herself and manage it easily.

Her choice wasn't really that hard to understand, or it wouldn't have been if she'd told anyone of the master astrologer's forecast.

Gemma had known her fate for years.

She'd told no one.

She'd sworn the astrologer to secrecy, and he had taken the truth to his grave.

Her HeartKeeper was the Prince of Regalia who would be king, the son of Queen Arcana whose true nature was disguised. She'd wondered about the prophecy when Drakina had been betrothed to Canto, but that prince's death had made everything more clear. Urbanus was the crown prince, so would eventually be king of Regalia. Although she was skeptical that his true nature was better than what she'd seen so far, Gemma had to believe a master astrologer.

She had to trust in the prophecy.

Astrologers, after all, were inclined to put great value in nuance. Gemma assumed that Urbanus was slightly less wicked than she'd come to believe. Maybe he thought he had good reason for seeing Arista assassinated and for trying to have Drakina killed, too. Maybe he was trying to gain his mother's favor so she ensured his succession, and he intended to mend his ways after her death and his coronation. Gemma might have been more inclined to help with such a goal if he hadn't ordered the death of her Sword Sister and best friend.

Maybe the Carrier of the Seed for Gemma wasn't the same man as her HeartKeeper. It didn't happen often, from what she understood, but that didn't mean it was impossible.

Either way, marrying Prince Urbanus was Gemma's destiny.

For better or for worse.

If it had been anyone else listening to their argument, Drakina would have noticed. Gemma's training made her more stealthy than anyone else—and Drakina's concern for Troy had become consuming. He was increasingly impatient and filled with restless energy. The situation had grown worse each day they had been on Incendium, despite her efforts to manage her father's expectations and her husband's desires. She knew it irked Troy to have so little to do, but a Consort *was* a ceremonial role.

That was why she knew they couldn't remain. Troy had investigated Incendium, spending much time in the starports, learning and making suggestions. He had been using the gym to excess, burning off his frustrations, and the results were most impressive.

Drakina had chosen duty and her father's will because she believed there wasn't really a choice. It had been her duty to conceive the heir to the throne. With each passing day, though, and her obligation fulfilled, it was increasingly clear that she had to do something to ensure the survival of her marriage. She, Troy, and Gravitas were finally going to Terra, immediately following Gemma's wedding. In a real sense, their shared future would finally begin, because their royal duties would be complete for the moment.

It was time to reassure her beloved.

Troy glared at her and Drakina had a sudden idea how that might be done. It frightened her a little, but the possibility of losing her HeartKeeper frightened her more.

"How can you ask whether I love you?" she asked, tempering her tone. "Of course, I love you. I am going to Terra with you, specifically so you can use your powers and be who you are. It is no small thing to leave my world behind for yours!"

"Maybe it's only because of the verran," he countered. "Maybe it's about hunting, not about me."

"You know better than that."

Troy shoved a hand through his hair. "I thought I did. I'm starting to wonder, princess, and I know that's not good. I don't want to fight with you, but I don't want to be irrelevant either."

Drakina halted before him and framed his face in her hands. "Don't confuse me with my father," she whispered. She brushed her lips across Troy's mouth. He shivered and exhaled, but still held himself apart from her. She met his gaze steadily. "I love who you are and what you can do. You cannot be fully yourself here on Incendium. It bothers me more than it bothers you."

He lifted a brow. "I doubt that."

"Do you?" Drakina challenged in a whisper. She stared into his eyes and dared to say it aloud. "Then MindBend me and learn the truth."

Troy was visibly surprised by the invitation. "You want me to manipulate your thoughts?"

"I want you to read my thoughts and share yours with me. I want our thoughts to be as one."

"Usually MindBending is guiding thoughts in a specific direction."

Drakina arched a brow. "I researched your skill and found this possibility noted. Are you not prepared for the challenge of learning a new skill?"

She saw the glimmer of excitement in his eyes. "It's supposed to come from cultivating a connection with one other individual."

"Who better than your wife and partner? I can think of no better candidate than my HeartKeeper."

Troy grinned. "How far into your mind can I go?"

"As far as you want," Drakina said, although the possibility terrified her. "I am an open book to you now, for we are bound together." She felt his anticipation rise.

"No repercussions?"

"None."

"Even if I find a secret?"

"I have none from you. I might not be good at telling you everything, but if I have stories yet untold, they are omissions not secrets. We are one, Troy."

"You forbade me to MindBend you once," he reminded her, his gaze searching.

"I now think it a necessary and timely concession."

He sobered, his gaze searching hers. "You're afraid, princess."

Drakina nodded, disliking the admission of any weakness. She did like, though, that Troy understood her without MindBending. "But I trust you, and you need to know how much. I cannot think of a better way to demonstrate as much."

Troy's hands landed on her waist. "Princess!" He understood the magnitude of the concession she made to him and would honor it. This bond would be intimate and one that could not be severed, but would strengthen the connection between them.

Drakina smiled for him. "Go ahead and MindBend me, Troy. You can even feed my desire, if you want, although it's already burning hot." She took a deep breath. "Remind me of the merit of slow and thorough."

He kissed her then, his delight making her heart skip.

"I was thinking fast and hot might be the right choice tonight, princess." His voice was a low rasp against her ear and the sound made her growl with need.

"I'm yours, Troy, all yours, whichever way you want me."

"Now there's an invitation I can't refuse."

"I was hoping it would be," Drakina whispered, then she felt his thoughts slide into her own. It was much as it had been that first time on Terra, but Troy was careful instead of stealthy. He let her be aware of him, and she welcomed that. She leaned her brow upon his shoulder and took a steadying breath, surrendering to his presence in her thoughts when her instinct was to incinerate the intruder.

"Okay, princess?" Troy didn't speak aloud, but his voice echoed in her own mind.

She tried to reply in kind. *"All yours, HeartKeeper."*

"Which creates some very interesting possibilities," he mused. She could hear laughter in his tone, even as it echoed within her mind, and she smiled at that. His fingers slid up her spine and into her hair, his touch sending tingles from her nape.

"You like that," he said, his thoughts a lazy drawl that tangled with her own thoughts. Drakina sighed with pleasure as the heat built within her. He threaded his fingers into her hair, moving slowly and deliberately. Drakina shivered in anticipation, welcoming the brush of his lips on her ears.

"And that."

"You know all of this already, MindBender," she thought. *"Dig deeper."*

Drakina felt Troy's surprise and guessed he'd discovered a little fantasy she'd been cherishing. She smiled when he embellished it with some variations of his own. He was kissing her neck and teasing her nipple when she made the fantasy much more naughty than any game they'd ever played before and she heard his laughter.

"Naughty, naughty, princess," he chided, but Drakina wasn't fooled. His pulse leaped and his breath caught, his body so taut with enthusiasm that she wanted to devour him.

Then Troy modified her fantasy and Drakina inhaled sharply at the allure of his suggestion. She seized the back of his neck, kissing him with a fervor that showed her approval. He backed her into the wall and their pulses raced as one as they kissed and caressed, then they fell on the bed with limbs entangled. Drakina braced her hands on either side of his shoulders and looked down at him, smiling at his obvious pleasure.

"You like this," she accused.

He nodded. *"But more importantly, I love you."*

After Drakina bent to claim Troy's lips in a fiery kiss, no one said or thought anything coherent in the royal apartments for quite some time.

That evening, Gemma strode down the corridor to the briefing session that she'd ordered, ensuring that she arrived precisely on schedule.

It was held in her own apartment, at her command, because that was the one place she knew was secure from spies and listening devices.

Some of the party from Regalia had already arrived to prepare for the royal family's attendance of the wedding the next day. Urbanus remained in his mother's palace on Regalia, per tradition, so there was no chance of the bride seeing the groom. The staff from Regalia were contained in one wing of the palace on Incendium, and Gemma doubted they had the skill to circumvent the access coding on their keys.

At least not so quickly as this.

Kraw bowed when she entered the unit and Farquon

saluted. Kraw was viceroy of the Kingdom of Incendium and had been in the service of King Ouros for decades, ever since his father had resigned the same post. His mustache had been as long and elaborately curved for all the years Gemma could remember him, but now it had turned white.

Farquon was commander of the regiment assigned to the defense of the royal family. Gemma had augmented Farquon's training herself, when she had led Incendium's elite corps of commandos. The assignment of a royal family member to military command hadn't been ceremonial for Gemma. She had trained on Cumae, graduated with high honors, then returned home to serve the kingdom. Under her command, the commandos had improved their response times, stealth, and kill rates. Farquon had been her best pupil, her lover, her friend and remained one man she trusted completely. She particularly admired that their relationship had never been complicated by talk of undying love.

Farquon had made the arrangements for her pending escape, and she knew he wouldn't reveal a syllable of her plan to anyone. Even now, he was completely impassive, commanded by Kraw to attend, and apparently without any greater bond to Gemma than to any other member of the royal family. He looked slightly bored if attentive. She felt a surge of pride in his talents, then inclined her head to Kraw.

"Your highness," Kraw said with a deep bow. "Your father sends greetings."

"Of course."

"As well as the reminder that you need not proceed with this marriage."

"But I must, Kraw, as my father knows." Gemma sat down and spoke crisply. "I'm sure he smells the Seed on every messenger from Regalia as keenly as I do."

Kraw inclined his head in acknowledgment of this

truth. "You need not go alone, Highness."

"I think otherwise." Gemma waved a hand. "Speak to me of Regalia, please, Kraw."

The wall illuminated behind Farquon, revealing that it was actually a large display screen. An image of Regalia appeared, undoubtedly captured by one of Incendium's satellites. As the image grew more detailed, it was clear that the surface of Incendium's sister planet was almost entirely covered in forest.

"A comparatively primitive world, it must be said," Kraw declared, turning to watch the display with Gemma. She always respected that he memorized his presentations, and made it look easy to present a wealth of information in a short period of time. "Their economy is heavily reliant upon barter on the planet itself, and simple skills. Their people harvest crops, make bread and ale, supply the royal palace with tithes and other offerings. Their major exports are medicinal herbs and other plants, usually dried for transport. They have only one star station, here in their northern hemisphere, near the queen's palace in their capital city."

The image showed a very small star station beside an extensive palace. A large dark shuttle was parked there, with loading doors of a size suitable for loading freight. There were only three more ships, all sleek and small personal vehicles. They seemed to have the royal insignia, though it was difficult to be certain. The palace was made of silvery stone that glittered in the sunlight and there were banners flying from its highest towers.

It was quite a contrast with Incendium's star station, where parking was always at a premium. There were dozens, if not hundreds, of small ships there at any given time, in addition to the regularly scheduled shuttles to the orbiting starport and the larger ships docked there.

"Their single shuttle leaves Regalia monthly and is an older model, somewhat prone to disrepair. They use

Incendium's starport to arrange transport of their goods to off-world markets." He paused to look at Gemma. "Without us, they would have no interplanetary access."

She arched a brow. "Our marital alliance could have practical benefits for Regalia."

"Of course." Kraw continued. "Their communication systems and general technology would be considered grossly inadequate by our standards. I fear you may have a difficult adjustment to make in your new home, Highness."

"But they have magic, don't they?"

"Magic." Kraw sighed. "Yes, that is their claim. The origin of the sorcery is the royal family, specifically Queen Arcana, whose abilities are said to be extraordinary. The power to cast spells, to glean the future, to enchant others against their will into doing her desire, to inflict different forms upon others, to read thoughts, to kill with a glance—all these abilities and more are attributed to the queen by rumor and gossip. It is said that she has given individual magical talents to her sons, allowing only one per offspring in order that they would have to band together to defeat her. It is also said that she deliberately fosters dissent between them." Kraw spread his hands. "These are the recurring rumors. There is no way to affirm which, if any, are true, and which might be either illusion or utterly without foundation." He cleared his throat. "What we do know is that Queen Arcana has lived a very long time for a mortal woman and has not appeared to age for the past fifty Regalian years. She has borne twelve sons and did so in rapid succession between twenty-five and forty Regalian years ago."

"And Regalian years are only a little longer than our own, I believe?"

"Yes, Highness. Their orbit is slightly larger than ours, giving us a warmer climate, too. The discrepancy between Incendian years and Regalian years is rounded to four per cent, and beyond the notice of most." Kraw bowed. "Certainly to an individual of your longevity, Highness, it is of little consequence."

Gemma nodded understanding.

The display changed to show images of men. Some of them were official holograms and familiar to Gemma, while others, she had never seen before. She recognized Canto, for example, before Kraw gestured dismissively to Queen Arcana's oldest and now deceased son. "It is unknown what magical power Canto might have had, at least here on Incendium."

"Whatever it was, it doesn't seem to have helped him much."

"Indeed, Majesty. You are familiar with Urbanus, of course," he continued and Gemma considered the official hologram of her betrothed. He was handsome, with his dark hair and blue eyes, his confident smile. "You may not be aware that he had a twin brother, Venero."

There was a roguish quality about Venero, whose hair was lighter than that of his brother. He had hazel eyes that looked almost golden. The image was a candid one, far more appealing than an official one. He looked to be on the verge of laughter as if he had been caught at some jest. Gemma had the urge to smile back at him and wish she'd heard the joke.

"They don't look like twins."

"Not identical twins. There was a suggestion—" Kraw cleared his throat "—that they did not share a father, although the sexual proclivities of the queen are beyond the range of our discussion."

That piqued Gemma's curiosity and she felt Farquon flick a glance at her. With an effort, she remained impassive. "You speak of Venero in the past tense."

"Prince Venero is said to have disappeared and is believed by most to be dead. It must be noted that

Urbanus has always been a favorite of his mother's. More than one observer has speculated that she wished his path to the crown to be unobstructed, particularly after the death of Canto, and that she had some involvement in the disappearance or death of Venero."

"Do you know about Urbanus' magical power?"

"Your betrothed, Highness, is rumored to be an expert in the making of potions." Kraw looked stern. "It might well be that there is no sorcery involved in this, merely an understanding of the effects of certain substances upon the body of the victim. It may be science disguised as magic, to defend such powerful and potentially harmful knowledge."

"Anything else?"

"Prince Urbanus appears to be quite involved in his mother's administration of Regalia, and also her confidante. I would guess that she is grooming him for the succession, as is right and good. He does leave Regalia at intervals and has been known to frequent the gaming halls of Xanto."

"He likes to bet," she said.

"Evidently, Highness."

Gemma wasn't impressed by that, but then, she wasn't going to be married to Urbanus very long if everything proceeded according to her plan.

The display changed again to an image of a heavily forested area. There was a dark spire in the middle of the forest, and it was enlarged as the focus tightened upon it. "There is new construction in the far southern hemisphere of Regalia, about as far from Queen Arcana's palace as might be possible without entering the inhabitable zones of the poles." Gemma leaned forward, avidly studying the structure. "This is said to be the honeymoon palace of Prince Urbanus." Kraw turned to face her. "It appears that your betrothed, Highness, intends to keep you to himself for a while."

Gemma's gaze danced over the palace as the view circled around it. It *was* a fortress, remote and structured to be easily defended, which suited her very well. She smiled for Kraw. "It looks like a perfect place to ensure the delivery of the Seed."

Never mind an ideal place to kill her new husband and escape Regalia without being observed. Gemma couldn't have planned it better herself.

She glanced up and Farquon bowed slightly, but not quickly enough to hide the understanding in his eyes.

All was made ready.

Let the nuptial festivities begin.

Chapter One

Prince Venero didn't attend his brother's wedding.

Even though it was to be a lavish ceremony and the union of the two kingdoms within their solar system was of key diplomatic importance, Venero had several reasons for missing the ceremony.

First, the vows would be exchanged on Incendium, and he had no means of getting to Regalia's sister planet, seeing that he had been banished from his mother's court and lost all the perks of living there.

Secondly, he hated Urbanus and had no wish to witness any joy his twin might experience.

Thirdly, Venero didn't think much good of the bride, Gemma, even though he'd never met or seen her. Any woman who would willingly marry the crown prince of Regalia had to be either stupid, or just as vile as Urbanus. Never mind that she was a dragon shifter. Venero couldn't imagine why any man would marry a woman who could slaughter him so easily that she didn't even have to wait for him to be asleep.

Women should be beautiful and demure, while wives should be beautiful, demure, and fertile. He supposed that Princess Gemma might possess the third trait, but not the others.

Venero was, however, very interested in the nuptials.

More specifically, he was interested in using the bride

for his own purposes. She might never know the difference if she was as dumb as he suspected. The fact that Gemma was a dragon shifter meant she was able to cover large distances quickly.

And Venero had a long way to go.

He wasn't just exiled from the court: he'd been cursed to take another form *and* had his powers suppressed. Worst of all, the antidote was something Venero knew to be impossible. How could he be restored to his human form by the kiss of his one true love when he didn't believe that kind of love existed?

Venero would solve that riddle later. First, he had to get out of the forest and back to the city of Regalia, where there were far more women—and thus more candidates for saving him.

Being a toad, however, didn't provide many options for quick journeys. The city of Regalia was hundreds of leagues away, but toads make slow progress and this part of the planet was particularly treacherous. The forests and rivers were full of predators with a taste for small amphibians, and Venero knew that wasn't a coincidence. Trust Urbanus to be vengeful. Venero hadn't been able to cast dreams to anyone since he'd been cursed, which made it hard to get any help.

Urbanus was nothing but thorough when he'd been cheated of whatever he thought was his due. Venero's brother had wanted to ensure his death, without getting his own hands dirty. Urbanus probably thought Venero was already dead.

But Venero had a surprise for his brother.

With any luck, Urbanus wouldn't discover the truth until it was too late.

The only good thing about the wedding was that Urbanus had built a remote castle, specifically to enjoy the pleasures of his new wife in privacy. As soon as Venero had heard about the castle, he'd known it offered him a chance. Sooner or later, the happy couple would return to the city of Regalia, and somehow, he was going with them.

Urbanus' new bride just might be dumb enough to help.

Venero had heard the hammering and the felling of trees, the lugging of stones and the long hours of construction. That the new palace was being built in the same region of Regalia where Venero had been dispatched just added to his conviction that Urbanus thought him dead.

Or powerless.

It had taken every bit of strength and resolve that Venero possessed, but he had made it to the castle by the day of the wedding. He doubted there would be another opportunity for release anytime soon, so he had to seize this one. He was exhausted when he hopped onto the path leading to the gates and took a moment to survey the creation. The new castle was a tall, slender tower and he grimaced at his certainty that the bridal suite would be at the top.

There'd been no time to delay, much less to rest. Venero had slipped through the gates, squirmed under a door, and started the ascent in the quiet castle. There were servants in the kitchen, but not many of them by the sound—and they weren't very happy with their situation, either.

He had been a third of the way up the endless winding stone staircase when he had a stroke of luck: a maid hurrying past with a basket of provisions was too busy grumbling to pay attention to her surroundings. Venero leaped as she passed and landed in the basket, then quickly hid beneath the folded cloth.

It was a bumpy ride, but one that saved him a lot of trouble.

He thought about kissing the maid in his relief.

Then he remembered the antidote and wondered if it was worth a try to seduce her. If Urbanus could have planned true love, Venero would have given the idea more consideration. His brother would have been amused to match him to such a woman, but surely there was something that escaped the control of his family's magical powers.

The maid abruptly unlocked a door at the summit, heaved a sigh, and pushed the basket into the room. He still might have given it a try, but a woman called from the foot of the stairs. She swore and locked the door again, leaving him alone.

The enormous draped bed told Venero that he had reached his destination.

It also reminded him that the maid might scream if he revealed himself. If she told Urbanus there was a toad in the palace—and why wouldn't she?—Venero would be caught. Urbanus would guess which toad, and this time, he wouldn't leave Venero's demise in doubt.

He'd only need a rock.

With a shudder, Venero slipped beneath a carved bureau with so many drawers that there was only just space beneath it for a toad. He caught his breath as he hunkered there in the shadows. He closed his eyes for a moment, but didn't dare fall asleep.

He could sleep in Regalia city.

The maid returned and made the bed with fresh linens, then opened the doors to the balcony. He could smell the forest far below.

Soon, the newlyweds would arrive.

Venero needed a plan.

Venero was beyond impatient by the time he heard the Starpod land in the bailey. Should he charm the bride? Should he encourage her sympathy? Or should he provoke her? Or should he just hide in her belongings?

Moments later, a woman entered the chamber accompanied by the maid. The maid bustled around the chamber, turning down the bed and opening the doors to the balcony even wider. Venero could see her clearly, on the far side of the room, but only the bride's shoes. The maid unpacked a small bag, leaving a fine chemise on the bed. The bride stayed beside the door.

There was no other baggage than the small bag, which the maid didn't put down. It defied Venero's belief that a bride would arrive with only the clothes on her back, but maybe the rest hadn't been brought to the chamber.

Maybe it wouldn't be.

Maybe Urbanus distrusted his bride.

Or wanted her close to naked most of the time.

Either way, hiding wasn't going to work.

Gemma still hadn't moved from the door. She seemed to be very still. Venero crept forward to steal a glimpse of her. Maybe that would help him decide on a plan.

The shocking thing was that she was beautiful.

Venero was hardly immune to feminine allure. In fact, he considered himself somewhat of a connoisseur, but he had never seen a woman as gorgeous as Urbanus' bride. He felt a sudden—and very inappropriate—interest in his brother's new wife.

She was blond and blue-eyed, curvy and of just the right height for a man to tuck against his side. She was exquisitely pretty.

She looked demure.

It didn't seem unreasonable to imagine that she might be fertile.

Of course, she was a dragon shifter.

The expression on her face didn't hint at vast intellectual powers. Venero recalled his earlier theory and thought both Gemma's expression and her situation confirmed it. Such a royal beauty must have had many choices of suitors. Why accept Urbanus?

Maybe her father had insisted upon the marriage.

But then, any woman with a bit of spirit would have protested a match that she didn't want herself.

She examined her wedding ring with apparent fascination, smiling as she turned it so the faceted stone caught the light. She giggled when it flashed. She repeated this gesture over and over again. The maid had to ask her three times whether she needed anything else before she appeared to understand the words, then she just shook her head.

Dumb as a rock.

Venero recoiled when a creature padded into the chamber and mewed at Gemma. She gave a cry of delight and bent to scoop up the beast, which had fur of a familiar blue and green combination.

A pavofel! Venero grimaced in distaste. That Urbanus' bride had anything in common with Queen Arcana couldn't be a good thing.

The maid left with the small bag, muttering, then Urbanus himself rapped on the door and swept into the chamber. "My lady!" he said and bowed low over her hand. Gemma fluttered her lashes, and Venero's heart clenched at her pretty vulnerability.

He'd obviously been hopping around the forest too long.

"I shall return shortly, my love," Urbanus declared, bowing and leaving the room.

She waved her fingertips at him. "Don't take too long!" she called after him, her voice breathy and pitched high.

The sound did strange things to Venero's pulse. The sooner he got back to his real form, returned to the city of Regalia, and indulged in some female companionship, the better.

To his surprise, when the door was closed behind Urbanus and the lock turned, Gemma's posture changed completely. She pivoted to stare at the door and Venero swore he could hear her attention crackle. She was suddenly alert and coiled to spring, so different from the bride playing with her ring that he blinked.

What had happened? Instead of a silly and lovely bride, she looked over the room with a gaze as keen as that of a hawk on the hunt.

No. Like a dragon on the hunt.

Venero shuddered.

Gemma dropped the pavofel, which leaped onto the bed and curled up there, eyes bright. She tried the latch surreptitiously, silently. She didn't knock on it or demand release, but simply pivoted to study her prison. He had the sense that she looked for a weakness, or a vulnerability she could exploit.

He eased forward, fascinated. Her eyes narrowed, but Venero could see their furious glitter. Like faceted sapphires, or snow in the sunlight. He had a definite sense that she was dangerous.

Gemma looked braced for battle, even though she carried no weapon. Her menacing expression made him retreat a little, for the sight reminded him that she was a dragon shifter.

Maybe a hungry one.

Did dragons eat toads? He had to think that they ate whatever they wanted.

Her survey complete, Gemma marched to the balcony. She moved with the lithe grace of a warrior, and Venero couldn't help watching her. She examined the space quickly. Efficiently. Venero understood what she was looking for, because in her place, he would have been looking for a means of escape, too.

Gemma looked over the rail to the ground below, and he guessed that she was judging the distance. She looked up to the peak of the tower, then strode back into the room. She tested the strength of the pillars of the bed, silently opened drawers, peered behind mirrors and drapes and appeared to inventory the contents of the chamber with calm purpose.

He was surprised to have anything in common with her.

Urbanus would be even more surprised.

Come to think of it, Gemma reminded him of Arista.

But the way her head turned and her eyes lit at the sound of the key in the lock as the maid returned was pure dragon.

The strange thing was that his inappropriate attraction to his brother's bride hadn't diminished a bit. In fact, he was even more intrigued by her—and more aroused—then he had been at first glimpse.

That must be the result of having been enchanted for so long.

He would have liked to have watched her disrobe, but the maid bustled her behind a screen, complaining of the draft from the balcony.

Funny how he had a lot more interest in soliciting a kiss from Gemma than from the maid. Maybe she could help him. Maybe she'd do it willingly. Maybe it wouldn't hurt to ask. He didn't think for a moment that she was his true love—he was sure there wasn't one, in fact—but a kiss from Gemma would suit him just fine, even if it didn't change his form.

Venero reviewed his possible plans. He didn't think he could win the sympathy of a dragon warrior. Given her fierce expression, he wasn't sure Gemma could be charmed. She looked like she'd take a challenge and run with it, though.

Venero smiled. Provocation, it would be.

And maybe a kiss for luck. His heart skipped at the prospect. Venero hunkered down to wait for his moment.

Finally, the worst was over.

Another bride might have thought otherwise and believed the pageantry of her wedding to have been the highlight of the day, but Gemma wasn't a typical princess. She hated the fuss of royal functions and had barely endured her mother's obsession with her dress and her hair and every little detail. After the endless ceremony and the meal were finally completed, she and Urbanus had flown to a private palace in Regalia in his Starpod.

He seemed to like when she was foolish. He expected just about nothing from her and had no interest in actually talking to her. Any concerns she might have had of liking her husband or feeling sympathy for him had been dismissed.

She disliked Urbanus. Deeply.

Killing him would be easy.

Gemma had smiled and simpered at him, congratulating him on his skills, but really, he was a mediocre pilot. She'd have tossed him back to the flight academy before she let him fly even the worst heap in Incendium's fleet.

All the same, she was married to him.

But not for long.

There was only the dirty work to be done, but Gemma preferred seduction and slaughter to ceremony.

The only complication was that the smell of the Seed was almost overwhelming. Gemma hadn't expected to be so influenced by it, much less to be distracted by it. The entire party from Regalia had reeked of the Seed on their arrival on Incendium, and Gemma had had a hard time keeping her desire in check throughout the day. The scent awakened her dragon and kindled her desire for lots of hot sex. She'd kept herself from ravishing Urbanus so far, but the longer the event was delayed, the more taut she felt.

The touch of his lips on the back of her hand made her simmer.

She hoped he wasn't expecting her to be a timid virgin.

It didn't seem to matter that she didn't like him. The Seed filled her senses and made her ready to claim it.

Gemma could only hope that her senses returned to normal once the deed was done.

When the maid left the second time, Gemma was alone for a precious few moments. There was no telling when Urbanus would return, so she tried to forget her lust and studied the chamber with care.

Her dragon didn't like that Urbanus had brought her to a private palace. Her dragon didn't like that the door had been locked behind her. Gemma didn't care for the fear in the eyes of her husband's servants, or his smug assurance that she must be desperate to consummate their nuptials. Her dragon didn't like her odd sense that she was being watched.

Gemma particularly didn't like that there was so little in the room that could be used as a weapon when she was in her human form. She felt out-maneuvered.

By a man who was a mediocre pilot.

No, he'd gotten lucky. The palace had been recently built and was scantily furnished. He hadn't thought much beyond the bed.

And she'd out-maneuver him before the evening was done.

Gemma exhaled. She had to make Urbanus forget her dragon nature, the better to surprise him when it mattered.

She stood alone on the balcony outside her bridal chamber, waiting for him. Her long fair hair was still braided into a single plait, and the hem of some sheer bit of nothing chosen by her mother fluttered around her ankles.

She posed herself and let her heart fill with her hatred of her new husband.

The shadowed forest spread beneath the balcony where she stood and the night sky sparkled with stars. It was funny how Regalia seemed to be so much more remote than its sister planet of Incendium, how its forests seemed darker and its solitudes deeper. Even though Kraw had shown her all of this, she hadn't grasped how isolated it was until she stood in the palace herself. The absence of communication systems and the lack of her own computational devices made her feel naked. Vulnerable. She could have fallen off the edge of the universe.

Where no one would hear her scream.

At least she had her fighting skills to rely upon.

Never mind her dragon powers. A woman who wasn't a shapeshifter would have been completely at Urbanus' mercy. Gemma remembered the royal family's reputed taste for spell casting and her spine straightened just a little. She wouldn't be beguiled.

Her plan was perfect, after all. She would seduce Urbanus and when he slept—as men always slept in the aftermath—she would kill him to avenge Arista. She would then shift shape and flee this remote palace, returning by night to the Starpod that Farquon had supplied and hidden at her command.

By the time the sun rose in the royal court of Incendium, Gemma would be gone, her destination unknown, her mission complete. She'd return only when her son's egg had to be delivered to the royal nursery. By then, she had to hope that the diplomatic storm would have spent its course.

It would be easy.

It would be over soon.

Maybe she should take Farquon with her for

company. Gemma would decide when she was back on Incendium. If he was there at the hidden Starpod, waiting for her, she'd invite him along. If he wasn't, she'd continue without him.

In a way, the remote location chosen by Urbanus was a benefit. There were fewer people who might witness her departure than would have been the case at the main palace. There were fewer who might come to Urbanus' aid, if *he* called for help.

Maybe he facilitated her scheme without even knowing what he did.

She smiled as Felice wound around her ankles, her tail flicking. The creature always knew when Gemma was agitated, no matter how well she hid it. Gemma bent and picked up Felice, stroking her brilliant blue green fur as she nestled close. Felice's eyes were bright green and she was of considerable size for a domestic feline, as well as a skillful predator. Felice sat on the rail surrounded by Gemma's arms and purred contentment. The sound and the vibration was soothing.

"Is this the part where you live happily ever after?"

Gemma spun at the sound of an unfamiliar male voice. That the words were tinged with scorn made her eyes narrow. The chamber was empty, the candles flickering and casting shadows on the walls. "Who's there?" she demanded.

"No one you know," continued the voice. There was no sign of movement in the chamber. "Call me a friend." Then he chuckled, as if nothing could be further from the truth.

Gemma was both intrigued and annoyed. What kind of chamber had she been assigned, that another person could be hidden within it? What game was Urbanus playing? Had she been watched as she washed and changed by someone other than the maid? It didn't sound like the maid's voice.

No, the voice sounded masculine and audacious. Challenging. The maid had been both female and meek.

The owner of this voice wasn't meek at all. Gemma was intrigued.

"A friend would show himself," she challenged.

"Maybe you just can't see for looking," came the reply.

Gemma dropped Felice and stepped into the chamber. She scanned every nook and cranny, peered into the shadows and up at the rafters.

No one.

"Don't you believe in happy endings?" Gemma asked, hoping to fool him into revealing his location.

"No, but then I don't believe in true love, either."

"Why not?"

"It doesn't exist."

"What a terrible thing to say to a new bride."

"Even if it's true?"

"It's not true. If it was, we couldn't each have a HeartKeeper."

"Maybe that's just a myth."

Gemma continued the argument as she sought the intruder. His voice was coming from one side of the room, where a large chest of drawers was pushed against the wall. "The astrologers would argue the matter with you."

"The philosophers, too. I still prefer to think for myself."

"If not to reveal yourself."

He laughed. "I'm in plain sight. Maybe dragons aren't so perceptive, after all."

Gemma felt her temper rising and guessed that her eyes were filled with fire. They always revealed when she was on the cusp of change. She tried to quell her reaction, knowing that the sight would remind Urbanus of her true nature. Her dragon was becoming ascendant at exactly the wrong time, thanks to this meddling individual. "Who are you and where are you? I demand that you show yourself!"

"Shouting is a great choice," the voice noted. "That way, Urbanus will know you aren't alone, and we'll both have to pay for that. Of course, he'll probably only see you." He sighed with forbearance. "I guess it's true that the dragon princesses of Incendium aren't very clever. But then, anyone who could imagine that Urbanus was her HeartKeeper must be a witless fool."

Gemma's inner dragon snarled, demanding release. She composed herself with an effort, but her temper kept simmering.

"There's nothing saying a dragon princess can only marry her HeartKeeper."

"But why would someone with every advantage accept anything less?"

Gemma wasn't going to answer that. "Where are you? Who are you?" she asked more quietly. She kept looking, seeking some sign of the intruder, but couldn't see him.

"A friend, come to warn you."

"With friends like you, I don't need of enemies."

He laughed again. "True enough." There was something very appealing about his laughter. It was confident, a little reckless.

Gemma wondered what he looked like.

The Seed made her burn to know more than that. "Warn me of what?"

"Of your husband, naturally. How much do you know about Prince Urbanus?"

"More than enough."

The intruder was skeptical. "I doubt that. How long have you spent alone in his company?"

Gemma hated that she had to admit a weakness. "Suitors of the royal princesses are closely chaperoned."

"No time at all then." The voice sighed. "At best,

you've barely scratched the surface of his nature."

Gemma's interest sparked. "Do you mean that his truth is hidden?"

"You could say that."

Urbanus was both HeartKeeper and Carrier of the Seed, then. Gemma couldn't dispel her disappointment. "Then what's your warning?"

"Watch his hands. He hides more than the truth."

"Like what?" Gemma waited, but there was no reply. "That's it?" she demanded.

"It's more than the warning I had," was the grim response. "He's coming. Don't be stupid enough to mention me."

"I won't," Gemma had time to say, although she wasn't sure why she made such a promise to someone hidden in her room. Could she trust him? Could she trust *anyone* in this place? It seemed unlikely.

The smell of the Seed meddled with her thoughts, making her more aware of her feelings than any logic. As far as Gemma was concerned, that situation needed to end as soon as possible. She hated being at the whim of her desires and bodily urges.

Impulse prompted her to listen to strangers.

She'd seduce Urbanus quickly.

Her heart skipped when she heard footfalls on the other side of the adjoining door. Her unexpected companion hadn't lied about her husband's arrival, at least. Gemma returned to the balcony. She scooped up Felice and resumed her earlier pose. Her heart was beating a little too quickly, but she doubted that Urbanus would notice.

Who was the intruder? Where was the intruder?

What was Urbanus' hidden truth?

Did it matter, if she had the Seed from him?

She had a sense of trickery that she couldn't avoid. Was it because of the warning? Or was the scent of the

Seed destroying her clear thinking?

Gemma heard the door open to the adjoining suite and gripped Felice a little tighter. Quick was the way to go. Quick and passionate and finished.

Then Urbanus would be finished.

"Gemma?" Urbanus asked, his voice making her jump.

"Urbanus," she replied, ensuring that her tone was welcoming. Her dragon snarled, but Gemma smiled.

Her new husband paused on the threshold. "What beauty in the night," he murmured, granting her an appreciative survey. "Like a beam of moonlight made flesh." Gemma averted her gaze, sensing that his words were insincere and not wanting him to see as much. He came to stand at the rail beside her.

Urbanus was taller than she was and not unattractive—at a distance. He was well-proportioned, but through the sheer white chemise, she could see that he wasn't muscled. He wasn't fat, not yet, but he was soft.

They wouldn't be married long, Gemma reminded herself, much less grow old together.

All she needed from him was the Seed.

She could still smell it, but oddly enough it wasn't stronger with his proximity. It had actually been more powerful in the chamber, but maybe he had spent time there, preparing the room for her.

Gemma had to admit that was unlikely.

Maybe the furniture had come from his own chambers.

Watch his hands.

Gemma considered Urbanus' hands and found nothing remarkable about them or their pose. They were a bit paler than she might have expected, as if he spent a lot of time inside. They were also unscarred. Undoubtedly he avoided the joust and other sports that proved a man's valor—in favor of what? Gemma didn't know. There was a signet ring upon his right hand and the wedding band now on his left. There was a little stain beneath the nail of his index finger, perhaps from the ink from signing the registry.

Maybe her so-called friend gave bad advice. She couldn't see anything worthy of note about her husband's hands.

She tried to sound welcoming, but guessed she would sound overly formal. "There is no need for flattery, Urbanus. We are married now and have exchanged our vows before thousands of witnesses." She thought she should warn him early, in case he liked virgins. "Even when I was a maiden, I knew what a groom was owed on a wedding night."

He grimaced as if to tease her. "Gemma, Gemma! Are we not *both* owed pleasure in the marital bed?" He stepped closer and put his arm around her waist. Gemma fought her urge to pull away. "Isn't that the point of the lessons we endure? To ensure that we can provide pleasure to our spouse on this night of nights?"

Had Urbanus been compelled to take formal lessons in copulation? Gemma bit back a smile. And she hadn't *endured* her nights with Farquon. She'd quite enjoyed them.

She dropped her gaze, letting him think she was shy. Her only pleasure would come from his early demise.

Urbanus dropped his voice low. "I know our match was arranged and the terms negotiated, but that doesn't mean there can't be a little romance between us." He lifted her hand and kissed her fingertips, his eyes gleaming as he watched her. Felice's purr sounded a little more like a growl, but Urbanus ignored the creature.

His hand felt fleshy and cold, and Gemma barely kept from pulling her hand away. Even the Seed wasn't helping. She had to be sure Urbanus didn't have any suspicions! She deliberately thought of Farquon and his great thick...

Urbanus bent and pressed a kiss against her palm. His lips were cold, too, and she fought a shiver. Gemma thought she felt a minute prick, then he folded her fingers over the spot he had touched with his lips. He held her hand captive in his left hand then, his right moving out of sight.

Had something happened? That warning resonated in Gemma's thoughts, even as a strange warmth surged through her. It seemed to emanate from the point Urbanus' lips had touched, which made little sense to Gemma. It made even less sense how she felt less resistant to the notion of their coupling.

She even felt more amorous.

Farquon seemed suddenly inadequate in comparison to her lord husband.

Gemma blinked. What had just happened?

Urbanus was watching her closely, more closely than she might have expected. Could he read her thoughts? No, no, it was Troy who was a MindBender. Urbanus was simply a royal prince.

Simply? The echo of doubt was dismissed so quickly that she might not have had it.

Gemma *was* a dragon shifter. The beast within stirred, and her passion surged. How strange that a kiss from Urbanus should provoke her passion. She tried to pull her hand back and open it, to look at the spot he'd kissed, but Urbanus held it within his own so resolutely that she abandoned the struggle. She didn't want him to think her reluctant.

"There are those who find love in arranged marriages," he said, his voice awakening a vibration within her. He drew her into his arms and Gemma let him. Oddly, his body felt good against hers, exciting even, and she felt her nipples bead. She forgot his chilliness, given the fire within her. Heat slipped through her veins, feeding her anticipation of their union, making her wet and ready.

It must be the Seed, calling to her body, awakening its destiny.

"Even happiness." His lips touched her shoulder then and his one hand slid to her shoulder. She felt another prick and another wave of desire, the heat doubling within her.

She tried to pull away but Urbanus trapped her between his hips and the railing. His lips trailed along her bare shoulder to touch her throat, even as he unbound her hair.

"Not both love and happiness?" she asked, and her voice sounded husky even to herself.

"They don't necessarily go together." Urbanus kissed her ear and Gemma was certain she had never felt such pleasure. Despite the fury in Felice's expression, she leaned her head back and closed her eyes, welcoming her new husband's touch. She felt his tongue, then his breath in her ear. "I loved my brother Canto but he didn't make me happy."

Gemma supposed it was inevitable that they talk about the situation that had brought them together. In a way, she respected that Urbanus didn't skirt around the fact that her sister had killed his brother. All the same, she didn't know how best to reply.

In fact, she was having a difficult time keeping her thoughts on anything other than his caress. The Seed was more potent than she'd ever imagined. She should have been warned!

His hands rose to cup her breasts then, his thumbs toying with the nipples even though the cloth. Gemma heard herself make a sound suspiciously like a growl, and Urbanus chuckled as he drew her away from the railing. Felice leaped down in disgust but for once Gemma didn't pay any attention to her pet.

"Beautiful ceremony today," Urbanus whispered. He pulled her against him and she felt his erection against her belly. She yearned for his strength inside her as he captured her lips in a seductive kiss. Every reservation within her melted as he locked his mouth over hers and cajoled her to join him, using his tongue, his teeth, and his lips. Gemma felt as if her blood was on fire. She gripped his shoulders, then clutched at his hair, opening her mouth to him in surrender. He kissed her thoroughly, then broke the embrace with obvious regret, smiling down at her with sparkling eyes. "Your parents did a fine job with it."

For a moment, Gemma didn't know what he meant. Her mind was filled with thoughts of coupling and kissing, of the two of them sating each other and wasting no effort upon mere words.

"The wedding," he prompted.

"I believe your mother contributed to its success, as well."

"No doubt she did," he said, with an interesting tinge of bitterness. "But it's typical, isn't it?" Urbanus cupped her nape in his hand, tipped her head back, and kissed her beneath her chin. His lips burned a trail toward her nipple, which he teased with lips and tongue and teeth until Gemma wanted to moan aloud.

When had she burned with such need?

The Seed must amplify normal urges.

"I don't understand," she said, dismissive of conversation. Before Urbanus could reply, Gemma framed his face in her hands, backed him into the wall and kissed him with savage force. Her new spouse, instead of being appalled, met her touch for touch. He seized her buttocks and lifted her against him. Their kiss was passionate and hungry, and Gemma could feel the leap of his pulse beneath her fingertips, even as her own raced. His hands were under her shift, her knees were rising to his waist, their mouths were locked together in passionate fury.

Felice meowed with apparent disapproval but Gemma didn't care. She wanted the Seed and she wanted it immediately.

Chapter Two

I t was Urbanus who locked his hands around Gemma's waist and broke their kiss, putting distance between them. His eyes were sparkling and his breath came as quickly as Gemma's. She might have protested his move, but he put a finger on her lips.

"Don't you?"

Once again, Gemma had a hard time recalling the thread of the conversation. Her body burned for satisfaction, the Seed demanded to be planted, and she was impatient with Urbanus and his need to chatter. She tried to kiss him again but he evaded her.

She gave serious consideration to shifting shape, toasting him into submission, then having her way with him.

But it would be rude.

And it would put him on his guard, when she needed him to relax.

"I think you do understand, but you're not sure that I would share your view. Let's have honesty between us, Gemma. I think you believe that we have very little in common, but I know you're wrong."

Gemma was intrigued. "Do you?" she asked, then reached for his erection. He caught his breath when she closed her hand around his strength, and she watched his nostrils pinch in pleasure.

"I do," he said, a most enticing strain in his voice, then lifted her hand away. "And I'll prove it to you."

"Does it have to be now?"

Urbanus laughed. "Yes, but I'll be quick, my lustful bride." He reached for the tie at the front of her gown, and unfastened it deliberately as he spoke. "I think it's typical that you and I are left to clean up the messes created by our older siblings. It's the fate of the second child."

He opened her gown and smiled at her bared breasts, then placed his hands beneath the sheer garment and pushed it over her shoulders. This was progress. Gemma tipped her head back at the feel of his palms on her skin and shook her shoulders so that the gown fell to the ground. Urbanus made a murmur of satisfaction when she was nude before him, and his hands fell to her breasts. He kneaded the nipples between finger and thumb, making Gemma twitch with need. She reached for the tie of his chemise, making quick work of the knot.

"We're never seen to be as special or wonderful or praiseworthy as the first-born, no matter what our older sibling might do. And when that sibling fails—as Canto and Drakina *did* fail to secure the alliance between our two kingdoms—then the obligation to make it all come right falls to us. The second born."

Gemma only let him talk because it was clear he meant to have his say before she had her satisfaction. Her mind was filled with need, and she would do whatever was necessary to urge him toward their mutual pleasure.

She pushed his chemise over his shoulders, sparing a glance to his nudity. Why had she thought there was anything wrong with softness? "You didn't have to marry one of Incendium's princesses," she said, pressing a kiss to his nipple. His hands closed around her waist and he lifted her against him.

Urbanus laughed. "You don't know my mother well,

do you?" He bent, his words intent as he murmured into her ear. She was more interested in his erection and how she might coax it to be closer to the size of Farquon's most impressive member. "But understand, Gemma, that when it was made clear to me that I should do so, I didn't choose you because you were next in the lineage." He claimed her chin and compelled her to meet his gaze. "I chose you specifically because we are the same."

His eyes were a thousand hues of blue, more marvelous to behold than she had realized. His gaze was filled with a surety that echoed the conviction in her own soul. He must be right. They were the same. They were destined to be together because they had been made for each other. How had Gemma ever doubted the allure of her spouse?

Urbanus watched as he traced a line on her cheek with his fingertip. "We're both unafraid to do what has to be done, Gemma."

That was true enough.

"We're both bold enough to act for the greater good."

Gemma's growing sense that she and Urbanus had a great deal in common was unassailable. It was truth. Their bond was right. Warmth flooded through her from her heart, an overwhelming sense that destiny had been fulfilled.

The Seed called.

Gemma itched to have it within her.

Urbanus really should shut up.

But he kept talking. "You're here not just because your father negotiated the marriage, but because a royal astrologer declared that I am the Carrier of the Seed." Urbanus arched a brow and she was awed that he alone should have discerned the truth. "Am I not right?"

"You know you are."

"So, it's fated to be," he said and kissed her

lingeringly once again. "It's our destiny and our choice to save our kingdoms with a union and a son."

"Except that there's Gravitas now," Gemma said, reminding her of Drakina's son and the heir to the crown of Incendium.

Urbanus chuckled, his fingers sliding into her hair, his possessive grip making her shiver. "You've been listening to a MindBender," he accused, solemnity lurking beneath his playful tone. "I thought you would know better than to be so beguiled, Gemma."

Beguiled.

Yes. That's what she felt. The realization flitted through her thoughts, along with the reminder of that warning. Gemma recalled those two little pricks and the sensation they had sent through her. Kraw had said that Urbanus dealt in potions, herbal mixtures that provoked a physiological reaction in the victim. Then she felt a third prick, one on the back of her neck. She opened her eyes even as fire flowed through her veins and her body capitulated to Urbanus and his amorous assault.

"What have you done to me?" she asked, her words slow and her own voice almost unfamiliar.

"Ensured that you couldn't cheat me, my beautiful bride," Urbanus confessed with a smile. He lifted his hand and she saw the small brace on his thumb, one that held a tiny thorn in place. His eyes shone with satisfaction and she realized that there had been some toxin upon it. He flicked it from his finger and cast it into the forest far below, clearly proud of his deceit.

"We are the same, my Gemma," he whispered darkly. "Each intent upon our own objective to the exclusion of all others. Today, I won." He smiled. "I eagerly await your retribution."

Gemma should have been appalled. She should have needed vengeance. But instead, she was falling asleep, powerless against whatever toxin he had given her.

In that moment, something fell with a crash in the chamber beyond her own. Urbanus stepped back, his brow furrowed with concern.

"Who's there?" he called, stepping toward the connecting door.

There was another crash.

Urbanus thrust Gemma aside and strode to the door, flinging it open and returning to his own chamber. She barely heard the sound of the key turning in the lock, securing her in her prison once more.

She was going to fall.

She made it to the bed and collapsed onto the mattress before her knees gave out beneath her weight. Gemma rolled to her back, against her own volition. Her legs parted, seemingly of their own volition, and once in that position, she was powerless to move.

She had been enchanted.

Because she had failed to take the voice's advice.

And now it was too late. A languid tide rolled through her body, making it impossible for her to keep her eyes open or lift a hand—much less to kill her spouse.

Her perfect plan had been foiled.

And Gemma hated Urbanus more than she had ever hated anyone in her life.

Vengeance would be hers, Gemma resolved, and then she knew no more.

Something had to be done.

Venero had watched Gemma succumb to Urbanus' spell, despite the warning he'd given her. He was horrified by his brother's obvious intention of making his new wife helpless. The import of that couldn't be good.

And it was hardly a fair fight.

Independent of his own agenda, Venero had to save her.

He hopped quickly across the room and forced his

way through the gap beneath the door to Urbanus' bedchamber. It was a tight fit and he scratched his back getting through the gap, but there wasn't a moment to waste.

Once in the chamber, Venero leaped to a table and kicked a lantern to the floor. It hadn't been lit, but the oil had recently been refilled. The glass vessel shattered, making a satisfactory sound, and the oil spread across the floor.

"Who's there?" Urbanus demanded, his voice sharp.

Of course, he had locked the door to his chamber and dismissed the servants. There shouldn't be an intruder in his sanctuary. Venero eyed another table, its surface crowded with vials and vessels. It was a bit farther than his usual range, but he didn't want to jump down into the oil.

Urbanus might start a fire to be rid of him.

Venero heard his brother's approaching footsteps. He took a deep breath, gathering his strength, and leaped for the other table. He barely made it and didn't manage a graceful landing. In fact, he crashed into a number of glass items and sent them toppling. He barged through the rest, sending many of them crashing to the floor, then jumped off the far side.

He had to hide!

He made it to the shadow beneath the bed by the time Urbanus crossed the threshold. His brother was still, his gaze seeking the culprit in the shadows, and Venero eased backward just a little.

"It can only be you, brother mine," Urbanus whispered, and Venero's heart skipped a beat that he'd revealed himself. He didn't regret the choice, though. Urbanus had to learn that he couldn't have everything his way. "Show yourself willingly, and I'll be kinder."

Venero wasn't going to bet on that.

"I can coax you out," Urbanus said, his voice

melodic. "You know I can entice you to reveal yourself, no matter what you plan."

Venero remained completely still. He tried to close his ears against any spell Urbanus might cast.

His brother took another step and reached for a flint. Venero had time to fear that his brother would inadvertently start a fire and that all opportunity for his own salvation would be lost, along with Gemma's free will.

Then Urbanus slipped on the oil. He lost his balance, swore, and hit the floor with a thud. There was a loud crack.

Followed by silence.

Venero feared a trick. He waited half an eternity, but there was no sound from his brother. He crept out of the shadows, slowly, cautiously, only to find Urbanus unconscious on the floor, a trickle of blood on his temple.

Venero didn't wait to see more. He didn't have time for relief. He skirted the perimeter of the room as quickly as he could, squeezed under the door again, and leaped onto the marital bed. The princess was sprawled there on her back, snoring softly. Her position told Venero all he needed to know about his brother's plans for consummating the marriage, with or without the bride's agreement or participation. Even from their short acquaintance, he knew Gemma wouldn't sleep in such a vulnerable pose.

"Wake up!" he whispered. "This is our chance to escape!"

Gemma gave no sign that she'd heard him.

Venero jumped on her belly, to no visible response. He jumped again and again. He flicked his tongue against her cheek and even though it stuck for a moment before releasing and must have tugged the skin, she slept on. He pulled her hair, grabbing a tendril of it in his mouth and jumping as far as he could so that it tugged at the root.

Gemma couldn't be stirred.

Had Urbanus given her a spell to sleep for a thousand years?

His ineffectiveness was frustrating and infuriating. He couldn't just sweep her up and save her. He couldn't solve the situation. He couldn't even wake her up. Venero had never felt so powerless in his life.

He was giving serious consideration to the idea of kissing Gemma, right on the lips, even though he knew it wouldn't do anything to help his curse—but just because it might wake her up—when there was a sudden blur of blue and green.

The pavofel leaped to the bed beside its mistress. It crouched, tail lashing and eyes gleaming, and Venero didn't dare to linger. He jumped from the bed, barely escaping the pavofel's swiping paw, and fled to sanctuary beneath that chest of drawers. The pavofel followed and slashed beneath the chest with claws bared. Venero retreated so that he was pressed against the wall, apparently out of range of the beast.

He'd never liked pavofels, but this one, he hated with particular vigor.

It prowled around the chest and he had more than one heart-stopping glimpse of its bright eyes as it bent to peer into the shadows. Wretched beast.

Finally, it abandoned the hunt and returned to its mistress' side.

Venero peeked out but the pavofel was on the bed, watching him. The ends of its tail flicked, those eyes in the fur seeming to stare at him, too. Venero eased back into the protective shadows, hoping the princess awakened in the morning.

His first chance of escape in years couldn't be lost as quickly as this.

Could it?

• • •

Gemma awakened with a foul taste in her mouth. Her head was pounding. She was sleeping on her back, like a trusting child, not the warrior she knew herself to be. She sat up in a hurry, feeling vulnerable. She was still in the bridal chamber but she was alone. Even Felice was gone from the bed.

Where was Urbanus?

What had he done before he left?

Gemma didn't feel any different and couldn't smell any indication in the bed linens that Urbanus had consummated their marriage while she was drugged and out cold. She felt her eyes narrow as she surveyed the quiet room. She wouldn't have put it past him to do such a thing. What had changed his mind? She could still smell the Seed, and its summons was a persistent hum in her blood.

The door to the adjoining chamber was closed.

It was probably locked, too.

The hue of the light indicated that the sun had risen. How long had she slept? One night or more? She realized that she could hear Felice hunting somewhere in the chamber, so she wasn't completely alone. Gemma got quickly out of bed and checked the door to Urbanus' chamber.

Locked. Of course. The keyhole was blocked, as if he'd left the key in it.

She pressed her ear against the wooden door.

Silence.

She smelled lantern oil and frowned. Why was it so strong? Surely Urbanus hadn't retreated to his chamber to refill his lamps? She couldn't imagine him doing such a menial task, much less thinking it was more important than consummating their marriage. She dropped to the floor and tried to peer under the door but the angle was wrong and the gap too small.

Gemma stood and considered her own chamber again, then noticed that the maid had brought water for her. The realization annoyed her—someone had come into her chamber and she hadn't even noticed. That was how powerful his toxin had been. Anything could have happened and that made Gemma angry.

She flung her chemise across the chamber and washed with haste. The water was just barely warm, so it had been there for a while. Where was Urbanus? What was his plan? The worst part was that she'd been tricked by him and it was her own fault. That voice, whoever it belonged to, had warned her, and she'd *still* been enchanted. Gemma made a little growl of frustration as she scrubbed herself clean, wondering again why Urbanus had just left.

Their marriage was unconsummated, which meant, she supposed, that it could be annulled. It didn't do anything to help her avenge Arista, though.

"Well done," that voice declared, no longer as unfamiliar as it had been. "Didn't I warn you to watch his hands?"

"You did," Gemma snapped. "And I forgot."

"It's not entirely your fault," the voice said. "He started to beguile you at the altar. Maybe even before."

"How? How does he do it?"

"I don't think I can explain."

Gemma propped her hands on her hips and surveyed the room. "I think you should try."

There was no response. Apparently, the owner of the voice had abandoned her.

As Gemma braided her hair, she saw Felice slip behind one of the drapes that hung on either side of the window. The fabric moved as the pavofel stalked something. Felice crouched, there was a faint scuffle as if the intended victim made a run for it, then the pavofel pounced.

Something squeaked.

Gemma was disgusted. It figured that on Regalia there were vermin in the bedchambers, even in the palaces, given what a rat her husband was.

She'd find another way to avenge Arista. Enough was enough.

The door to the corridor was still locked from the other side. Only the balcony door could be opened, probably because it was accessible only from her chamber. Gemma smiled as she stepped onto the balcony, because Urbanus had forgotten one critical detail. There was a sheer drop of considerable distance to the forest below, but that was no obstacle to Gemma in her dragon form.

The sky beckoned.

She was out of this place.

"Come on, Felice," she said, more than ready to abandon her new husband. "Forget the mouse. It's time to go. Goodbye, friend, whoever and wherever you are."

There was no reply.

Felice bounded toward her, some unfortunate creature in her mouth, and Gemma summoned the shift from deep within herself. She should have been in dragon form, poised for flight, just as Felice leaped for her.

Except that nothing happened.

Felice collided with Gemma's upper arm and fell to the ground with a mew of displeasure. Gemma couldn't see or feel the shimmer that came before a shift. She tried again, with no better luck.

Was it because she'd been drugged?

Panic slipped through her, but Gemma was undaunted. She called imperiously to the change. She commanded her body to shift shape, willing it with all her might. This ability was her birthright and part of her nature, after all.

But still, nothing happened. She was standing nude on the balcony of Urbanus' palace in her human form. Even her nails hadn't changed.

What was going on?

"It won't work," that voice declared. "He must have planned it that way."

"I thought he forgot my abilities."

The voice laughed. "He doesn't forget anything." His laughter faded. "Well, maybe he forgot one thing."

"What?"

"Me."

Gemma looked around. There was no sign of the speaker. "Well, it would be easy to forget you since you don't show yourself. Maybe you're not even real."

"I'm real enough," the speaker insisted, then yelped. "Ouch!"

Felice spat out the creature she had caught, shook her head, and backed away. It was small, small enough to fit in Gemma's palm, and gray. It might have been a mouse, but it hopped. It didn't hop well, but crookedly, as if it had been injured. Felice batted it with a paw, as Gemma bent down to look.

It was a toad.

Its front leg was bleeding, and it hobbled behind the open door to take refuge, leaving a trail of blue behind it. When Gemma moved the door, the toad was examining the damage. There was something very untoadlike about the way it looked at the limb, then tested it and surveyed it again.

"I hate pavofels," the toad muttered, revealing the source of the voice that had given Gemma advice. Felice slipped behind the door, so sinuous that she might have been without bones. She stalked silently, eyes glittering, her intent more than clear.

Gemma scooped up her pet. Felice was too far away to strike the toad but tried anyway. "You're a toad and you talk!"

"I talk," the toad agreed grimly. "Take it as proof that you're not the only one who's enchanted."

"So, he *did* beguile me?"

"Aren't you sure?" the toad demanded, its tone skeptical.

Gemma bent down. "Why did he stop?"

The toad was actually many shades of silver and gray and green, and less unattractive than Gemma might have expected. Its eyes shone like amber beads and when it met her gaze, as it did in this moment, she felt as if it were almost human.

"Because I saved you," the toad said.

Gemma laughed. She couldn't help it. "You? Saved me?"

"And a very near thing it was, too." The toad glared at her. "You're welcome."

"How did you save me?"

"By distracting Urbanus. I broke a lantern in his room, so he went to find out who was there."

"Did he see you?"

"No. He slipped in the oil and hit his head."

Oh! Gemma felt herself blush. "Then I apologize. Thank you." She straightened, suddenly aware of her nudity. It shouldn't have mattered in front of a toad, but Gemma had a feeling that in this situation, it did. His eyes seemed to have gotten brighter. "I suppose you want a favor now, or a wish."

His tongue flicked and he chuckled. "How about a kiss?"

Gemma was disgusted. She stalked back into the chamber and cast Felice onto the bed. She pulled her chemise over her head.

"I suppose it *is* too much to hope for." The toad hopped after her, its tone indicating that he thought otherwise.

"It's frogs who are saved by kisses, not toads."

"Are you sure?"

"Yes!" Gemma straightened and turned to face the toad. She saw Felice crouching, intrigued by the toad all over again now that it was moving. "Who are you and why are you here?"

"I'm looking for help, of course." He lifted his foot. "Would you want to be a toad?"

"Then you're not really a toad?"

He sighed with forbearance. "Do toads talk on Incendium?"

"No, but there's no telling what's normal on Regalia. It is said to be a place where everyone in the royal family is a sorcerer."

The toad cleared his throat pointedly.

"Point taken," Gemma said. "But I can't help you, not trapped in this chamber."

"You wouldn't be trapped if you'd listened to me."

Gemma snatched up Felice just as the pavofel would have pounced on the toad. The creature protested loudly and the toad retreated, still trailing blood. "Are you hurt?"

"What do you think?"

"You don't have to be rude."

"And you don't have to be stupid," the toad replied, his irritability clear. "I thought the dragon princesses of Incendium were supposed to be smart." It gave her a look, then glanced down at another small puddle forming on the floor. "This would be blood. Blood flows when the body is injured. *Ipso facto*, I'm hurt."

"I didn't know toads spoke Latin."

"It appears that there's a lot you don't know."

"You don't have to be so cranky."

"Don't I? My advice was ignored by the one person who could help me, ensuring that she can't help me after all, and now I'm being mauled by her pet. Looks like it's true that no good deed goes unpunished."

Gemma considered the chamber, unable to argue with that assertion. "It does, doesn't it?" She flung Felice on the bed and the pavofel curled up, its disdain clear. "I'm sorry, and I'm sorry for Felice's hunting, too. Is there anything I can do for your leg?"

"Probably not."

"Will you tell me more about the spell?"

The toad puffed up, becoming almost double in size. Gemma thought it looked revolting. "I thought you'd never ask."

Felice leaped from the bed suddenly and the toad cried out as it was seized in the pavofel's mouth.

"Felice! NO!" Gemma cried and her pet dropped the toad, which hopped toward her a little less robustly than before.

"Thank you very much," the toad said. "Can't you restrain that thing?"

Felice hunkered down, eyes gleaming and tail swishing.

"That *thing* is my pet and maybe my only friend on this planet."

"Why? Because you listen to its advice? *We* could be friends, if you made a little effort."

Gemma took a deep breath. "Okay. You're right and I admit it. I *am* sorry. Now, can I break the spell or does it have to wear off? How do these things work?"

"Spells can work in a hundred different ways, depending on the intention of the spell caster."

"That doesn't really help."

"The question is what Urbanus defines as the greater good." The toad hopped closer. "And whether you're part of it, key to it, or an obstacle to it."

"Because I can guess what he'll do in each of those instances."

A groan came from the other side of the door to

Urbanus' chamber, revealing his location. The toad seemed to grin, as if satisfied with her husband's unhappy state.

"How badly is he hurt?" Gemma whispered.

"He's not dead." The toad sighed. "Clearly, wishes don't always come true."

How unexpected to have something in common with a talking toad, even if it was a dislike of her new husband.

Gemma folded her arms across her chest. "Okay. A quick introduction to spell casting, please. How do I break the spell and get my powers back?"

"With the antidote, of course."

"Which could be anywhere or anything depending upon the intent of the spell caster."

"Exactly."

"Do you know where or what it is, in this case?"

"I could guess, but I'm not telling until you help *me*."

Gemma bent down. "And here I am hoping that the antidote involves the sacrifice of a toad."

The toad, to her surprise, laughed although it was a rueful sound. "It just might."

"Why? Who are you really?"

The toad stretched up and Gemma realized it was offering its mouth to her. "One kiss and you can find out."

She bent and touched a fingertip to his forehead, considering it. But the feel of his skin made her shudder and step back in disgust. She took refuge in a technicality because his disappointment was almost tangible. "If you were a frog, I might. But everyone knows that enchanted princes don't become toads."

"You don't know Urbanus very well, do you?"

Gemma pivoted at the sound of a key in the lock to the corridor. The maid!

"Here's your only chance to get out of here," the toad muttered. "Do I have to explain it and can you figure it out all alone?"

"Oh, shut up or I'll leave you behind," Gemma had time to say before the door swung open and the maid entered the room. She seemed to be startled to find Gemma waiting for her, even though she carried a tray with a steaming bowl upon it.

"I trust you slept well, my lady?"

"I did, thank you," Gemma said with a smile. She acted like a fool, the better to win the girl's trust. "That smells delicious. Could you set breakfast on the balcony for me? I *love* the view of the trees! Look at the sunlight on my ring!"

Venero was impressed by Gemma. At the sound of the key in the lock, her manner changed completely. He could have been watching a different person than the woman he'd been arguing with just moments before.

He admired anyone who could play a role when necessary. He didn't like deceit much, but sometimes a small deception served the greater good. If the maid under-estimated Gemma, they would have a better chance of escape.

But it was more than that: he'd seen Gemma nude and he couldn't forget it. She was beautiful. Ideal, even. She had creamy breasts, which he thought to be the perfect size, and the way her nipples tightened in the cool morning breeze had been particularly distracting.

He'd wanted to touch her.

No, he'd wanted to caress her. He'd been sure he'd despise her, given her shape-shifting abilities, but the reaction Gemma provoked in him was the very opposite. He wanted her in all the ways he couldn't have her. And that was strange: he liked ornamental women as sexual partners, and skilled warriors as companions. He'd never met a woman who he admired in both ways. Arista, for example, had been a good companion and partner in battle, but he'd felt no sexual desire for her at all.

Of course, Arista hadn't really been a woman, so maybe that explained everything.

Venero's reaction to Gemma was so uncharacteristic that it confused him.

Maybe that was the result of his recent celibacy. Years as a toad had left him with many unsatisfied urges. Maybe any attractive woman would have provoked such a reaction in him. Maybe it didn't matter. Maybe he'd reward them both with a satisfying interlude after she helped him to earn his own freedom.

He hoped she got them out of here and soon.

Venero forced himself to listen and watch.

Gemma was all grace and solicitude, complimenting the maid so much that Venero thought she overdid it a bit. The girl blushed and beamed, though, more than happy to move a table for her gracious lady and get a cushion for the chair. She admired the ring at Gemma's insistence, and smiled at the way the light flashed in the stone. She set out the meal, barely noticing how Gemma moved behind her.

Venero blinked as Gemma incapacitated the maid, her attack as quick as lightning and more effective than he expected. The maid was struck and she fell, but Gemma caught her. She was stripped naked, gagged, and trussed helpless in the blink of an eye. She was unconscious but he guessed not injured.

He recognized the move from Arista. It was a trick of those trained on Cumae to stun a victim just long enough to see that individual bound, and it wasn't easily done. It required a perfect balance of force and gentleness, as well as meticulous timing.

As he watched, Gemma touched the maid's temple with a care completely at odds with the inflicting blow, a gesture Venero remembered well.

It had to be true, then, that Gemma had trained on

Cumae. It was part of the story of the royal family of Incendium that the second daughter of the king had trained on Cumae and led an elite regiment on her return to her home planet, but Venero had always thought it was just propaganda. He hadn't been able to believe that any princess would undertake that kind of physical challenge, much less succeed at it. Gemma's moves proved that she had done it and probably graduated at the top of her class.

He was impressed, so impressed that he almost forgot to watch Gemma dress.

Urbanus moaned a little more loudly then, recalling him to the situation. Venero hopped toward Gemma. "Hurry!"

The girl's lashes fluttered as Gemma was putting on her boots. The maid blinked and frowned, then wriggled as Gemma pulled the lavish coverlet over her.

"I am sorry," Gemma whispered. "It's my only way out. Are you quite comfortable?"

The girl nodded, her amazement echoing Venero's own. Gemma pulled her wedding band from her finger then and pushed it onto the girl's smallest finger. Her hands were more plump than Gemma's.

"Since you like it," Gemma whispered. "Sell it if you like."

The maid's eyes widened and Venero knew she'd never imagined that she'd even touch such a ring, let alone possess it.

But Gemma didn't look back. She seized the bucket from the water and the key from the door, then nudged her pet with her toe. As soon as she opened the door, the pavofel shot through the gap in a streak of vivid blue-green.

"Oh, my lady! The pavofel!" Gemma cried, mimicking the maid's voice.

"Me! Me!" Venero cried, but Gemma was already

scooping him off the floor with one hand. He felt her shudder of revulsion, then she dropped him into the pocket on the front of the maid's plain dress. There was a handkerchief there and it wasn't clean, which made Venero shudder with revulsion, then he jostled in the pocket as Gemma ran down the stairs.

At least she'd kept her promise. He found himself pleased with his companion.

"She wouldn't know the word," he felt obliged to point out.

"What word?" Gemma demanded in an undertone.

"Pavofel. We don't have them here, and she isn't a great reader."

"Do you think he heard?"

There was no point in lying. Venero sighed. "Yes."

Gemma swore with the vigor of a hardened mercenary, and Venero was astonished yet again by her. She then ran faster, galloping down the stairs with a wanton disregard for his comfort.

"Don't drop me!" he insisted, knowing he'd be smashed by the fall. Gemma closed her hand around the opening of the pocket.

Venero was jostled and bounced in her pocket but wished he could see her running. She had to be as graceful as the cervus he'd hunted on Sylvawyld during his incarceration there. They were such beautiful creatures that he'd always regretted his need for food and had never eaten their meat since.

Venero felt the change in the air when Gemma reached the ground floor, because it was cooler there, then heard her throwing open the bolts on the kitchen door. He smelled the herbs in the garden as she took the most direct path to the gate, and felt the heat of the pavofel when she scooped it up into her arms.

The miserable creature reached a paw into the pocket of the dress, and Venero tucked himself as far away from those claws as he could.

"Control your pet!" he cried.

"Because I don't have enough to do," Gemma complained. Even so, she lifted the pavofel higher, much to his relief.

He could see a patch of morning sky through the opening at the top of the pocket, then the branches of the trees on the perimeter of the forest etched against it. The skirt spun and he had to hang on to the lip of the pocket as Gemma turned back to face the palace.

And at the height of the tower, Venero saw a male figure, silhouetted on a high balcony. Urbanus.

"Oh no," Venero whispered.

"What's he doing?"

The crown prince raised his hand, scattering something into the wind, and Venero swore himself when he saw the glitter of spelldust.

Chapter Three

un!" Venero bellowed, but Gemma didn't need his encouragement. She had already spun to flee. She leaped over fallen branches and raced deeper into the forest, panting but never slowing down. He was amazed by her speed and her agility, and by her determination to outrun the spelldust.

But he heard Urbanus calling to the wind to aid him and Venero guessed that Gemma could hear it, too.

"What do I do?" she demanded.

"Keep it from touching your skin. Can you see it?"

"It glitters. What is it?"

"Spelldust."

She groaned. "Trust my luck that I end up trapped on a planet filled with magic." Her scorn was clear and intrigued Venero. "What does spelldust do?"

"It takes whatever it touches out of the time stream."

"What?"

"It immobilizes things, freezing them in one moment, either for eternity or until released by the spell caster."

"Anything?" Gemma sounded incredulous.

"Everything."

Gemma swore again. She splashed into a stream, and Venero saw the first sparkle of the dust descending. It touched the tree tops and they glittered, then stilled. It was a sight that Venero always found both fascinating and horrifying. Immortality lost any allure it might have had the first time he saw spelldust in action.

"Quick!" he urged. "Under the water."

Gemma didn't hesitate to take his advice this time, which was an encouraging change. She dove into a pool of water so quickly that Venero barely had time to take a deep breath himself. The pavofel was furious and yowled in protest, at least until the water closed over them all—then it fought wildly.

Venero was glad to see someone else injured by the creature. He saw it make a trio of long scratches on Gemma's arm, deep enough to draw blood. But Gemma remained calm, even as she wrestled the miserable feline. He had to admire that.

Venero would have been inclined to let it go, but Gemma hooked her ankle around a branch sunk to the bottom of the pool to keep herself below the surface, then blew into the pavofel's nose. This scarcely made the creature any happier, but it wasn't going to drown as Venero feared he might.

She solved problems without hesitation, and she didn't surrender without a fight. He liked both of those traits.

He might have felt more admiration for her in that moment, but the fabric of the dress swirled upward in the water and wrapped around him like a shroud. Venero was caught and only had glimpses of the opening at the top of the pocket. He sputtered. He thrashed. He wanted to remind Gemma that toads were not aquatic creatures, but she was busy with that stupid pavofel. Venero could feel her wrestling with it.

He'd never wished for his DreamCasting abilities with greater vigor than in that moment, but he knew they were gone.

Enchanted into oblivion, just like Gemma's shape-shifting powers.

Venero choked. He struggled in a bid to get Gemma's attention, hoping she might pull him free. The fabric caught at his legs as if it followed some instruction from Urbanus. He supposed that wasn't out of the question. Frustration rose within him even as he fought for air. He was drowning, still enchanted as a toad, and his front leg hurt.

Venero wasn't going to die this way, even if that might be his brother's preference.

It was about more than his own fate, though. Gemma wasn't nearly safe, and he felt a protectiveness toward her. She didn't understand magic or Urbanus, and she'd need Venero's help to survive—never mind escape.

Urbanus couldn't destroy them both.

When Gemma got out of the river, she would be cold and wet. She would need shelter and heat before she could continue to seek her antidote. Celo's hut would be the closest shelter, and even though Venero had promised to leave his youngest brother in solitude, he'd have to break that promise today.

For Gemma.

He gave a ferocious kick and heard the cloth tear. He silently thanked Urbanus for keeping his servants so poor that they had to wear their clothing to rags. He blew a stream of bubbles with the last bit of air in his lungs and lunged toward the surface in the same moment. He felt Gemma snatch after him, undoubtedly hoping to save him from the spelldust, and his heart swelled with more of that admiration. He evaded her grasp, probably only because she was fighting the pavofel. He swam without looking back, not wanting to see her fear for him.

As he anticipated, the spelldust was landing on the surface of the stream. It sparkled and glittered there in a hundred different colors, as if to entice them all to touch it.

Venero knew better. He spied a leaf floating on the

river, its stem dangling beneath it in the water. Maybe his luck was turning. He managed to grip the stem and let the current sweep him away, down the river, down toward Celo's hut. He pushed his head into the hollow beneath the leaf and took a gulping breath.

All he had to do next was accurately guess when to abandon the leaf and jump out of the river.

And convince Celo to help Gemma.

Venero wasn't sure which would be the greater challenge, but he was alive and that had to count for something.

He was on the bank before he realized that he was relying upon Gemma's resourcefulness. She'd save herself, now that he'd given her a hint of how to evade the spelldust. He had no doubt of it.

A demure beauty wouldn't have survived, much less been such a reliable comrade.

Venero decided to think about that later.

The toad!

Gemma had been so worried about Felice and the spelldust that she'd forgotten the toad in her pocket—at least until it thrashed free of her skirt and swam for the surface. She reached for it, but missed. The spelldust! Was it ignoring its own advice? She could only watch as it rose to the surface. It seized a floating leaf, though, and used it as a shield. It then disappeared from her view, swallowed by the swirling current of the river.

She supposed it had only wanted out of the castle and that once she'd helped it do that, there was no reason for it to linger. But she already missed its company.

Never mind its advice. Magic was all new to Gemma. They taught science on Incendium, and she had refined her fighting skills on Cumae. But she couldn't anticipate a sorcerer like Urbanus, because she didn't understand his powers.

That was annoying.

It looked like the spelldust was fading on the surface of the water. Although it might be smarter to wait a little longer, Felice needed air. The pavofel had stilled in her arms but she could feel its heartbeat. Gemma recalled the toad's strategy. She surged toward the surface and swam toward the bank.

To her relief, there was a rock that leaned over the water, casting the surface in shadow. She emerged beneath its shelter. Felice needed no encouragement to do the same, but Gemma had to forcibly keep the pavofel from leaping to the shore. Wouldn't the spelldust go through the pads of her feet? Gemma had to assume it would. Did it expire? Surely it followed some logical rules.

She wished she could ask the toad.

Gemma couldn't do that, but she could follow its example. She guessed that at some point downriver, there would either be no spelldust or its power would have waned. She tucked Felice tightly under her arm and considered the stream. It flowed fairly quickly here and she could see another outcropping a good distance downstream.

"Hold your breath," she told the pavofel, which gave her a simmering look of displeasure. Then she blew into Felice's nose again and ducked under the surface, swimming with all her might toward that outcropping. The current helped, and she reached it more quickly than expected. She chose another that was further downstream, and did it again.

Felice scratched her, of course, fighting her every moment that they were under the water. Gemma didn't care. She'd protect the pavofel to the end, even if it was a thankless task.

The pet had been a gift from Arista, after all.

The rhythm of swimming and catching her breath

gave her a chance to think. Arista had always said that warriors came in many guises and were armed with many different weapons. She ought to have known. She had been contracted as a mercenary for years in between her stints of teaching on Cumae.

Wouldn't Arista have considered Urbanus a warrior, as well? Gemma thought she might have done. Wasn't he fighting for what he desired, but using his own arsenal? He'd anticipated Gemma's own plan and disarmed her with his sorcery before she could execute it, and done so in order to see his own goals achieved. That sounded like war to Gemma.

Or at least a battle for supremacy.

She couldn't shift shape anymore, which was less than ideal, but it didn't mean she was helpless either. Gemma could fight back, or maybe even outsmart Urbanus, even in her human form.

The trick would be to anticipate him.

How could she do that without knowing his goal?

She thought about the toad's question. Was she part of Urbanus' plan, key to it, or an obstacle? She couldn't be an obstacle yet, because he would have simply killed her when he had the chance. He'd let her live, although he'd disabled her ability to shift shape. That implied that he still needed her, and that he wanted to control her until she fulfilled her usefulness to him.

She was pretty sure he'd intended to consummate their marriage, and would have done so if the toad hadn't saved her.

Did they share the goal of securing the alliance between Incendium and Regalia by marriage? Or did Urbanus believe that the child of their union would be able to save their twin planets from destruction? Or did he simply want to cement the alliance between their planets, given the reliance of Regalia on Incendium? If any of those were the case, he'd need her to survive at least long enough to bear their son.

He wanted to keep her on Regalia, that was clear, and under his control. Her dragon powers would have given her the ability to escape, so had to be undermined. Was her power gone forever? Gemma didn't want to think about that possibility, but it was worth consideration. She doubted that Urbanus wanted her to regain the ability to shift shape any time soon, if ever.

The toad had mentioned an antidote, which implied that the spell would hold unless she found the antidote. How would she find it without the toad's help? She didn't know nearly enough about either spells or Regalia. Her assumption that she wouldn't be on the planet long now seemed foolish.

She didn't blame the toad for expecting better of her.

Arista would have expected better of her, too. She'd let her confidence keep her from making contingency plans, and now she was in a predicament with no way to let anyone know. All her comm, even her interpreter, had been stripped away after the wedding ceremony. Urbanus had charmed her mother when he'd called them distractions to romance. Gemma had ceded, sure that she could triumph without them.

She was annoyed by her own gullibility. The truth was that she'd underestimated Urbanus, and that he'd used that to his strategic advantage.

She had to turn the tables on him and escape.

Without the toad's help.

Did all the toads on Regalia talk? Gemma thought not. Her toad had said it was enchanted. Who was it really? Had it been cursed by Urbanus, too?

Maybe she *should* have kissed it.

What Gemma didn't realize was that when she considered kissing the toad, she had touched him on his parietal eye, the mystic third eye also known as the pineal gland. It was in the middle of his forehead, marked by a white spot. Toads saw the world differently from men, but the fact that this toad was actually a man, and one from a family of sorcerers, meant that his parietal eye was particularly well developed.

The touch of Gemma's fingertip restored Venero's ability to send dreams.

As soon as Venero realized as much, he wanted to do more than kiss Gemma.

He realized it by chance, when a hawk swooped down toward him as soon as he reached the bank of the river. On impulse, Venero sent a dream to the hawk of a full belly. The hawk swooped down and scooped him up, and Venero feared that nothing had changed. But the hawk flew and flew, carrying him like a treasure, and he dared to believe again. He sent the hawk a dream of flying toward Celo's hut and dropping him there.

It worked.

Venero could have shouted with glee. Gemma had helped him regain his DreamCasting powers, which might mean that she could break the spell completely.

Maybe he'd misunderstood the notion of true love.

Maybe it was about admiration and respect.

Either way, his restored abilities saved him a lot of hopping, even if he was a bit bruised from the drop.

Venero had forgotten how good it felt to have some control over his own fate, never mind how easy it was to turn the thoughts of wild creatures to his will. He'd first used his skill with woodland creatures, then after practice, had turned to humans. His siblings were another level of challenge altogether.

Venero hoped his youngest brother would be of aid, although influencing Celo would be a greater challenge than tricking a hawk or a cervus.

Celo was exactly where Venero had expected him to be.

He was outside his little hut in the depths of the forest, chopping wood.

Venero's youngest brother didn't look much like a prince of the royal blood of Regalia. His hair was longer and his beard was almost to his waist. He was more muscular than Venero recalled, but he'd have to be working hard to survive in the old forest. That told Venero how determined Celo was to never go back to the palace.

Not that Venero could blame him.

Celo's axe fell with regular rhythm. Venero was exhausted but he hopped the last distance and leaped onto the woodpile.

"Well met, brother mine," he said, and Celo started.

He stared, then buried his axe into the chopping block and bent to look Venero in the eye. "Not you," he said grimly, which wasn't the warmest of welcomes. "Not again."

"Me. Again." Venero tried to smile. "Good to see you, too."

"Don't you ever give up?"

"Not in my nature, I'm afraid."

Celo grimaced and spared a glance upward. The trees were dense but far above their branches, the clear blue sky could be seen.

"I wasn't followed," Venero said.

"Yet," Celo noted and he had to concede that possibility. "You promised," Celo accused, folding his arms across his chest as he eyed Venero again.

"I did, and I apologize."

"And you've shielded your thoughts," Celo noted. "At least you haven't lost all of your powers." He lifted his brows. "Or maybe you've met your one true love. Is she beautiful? Demure?"

Venero didn't answer that. "There's a damsel in distress that I need you to help."

"The lady in question?"

"Urbanus' new bride."

Celo grimaced. "Isn't she in the tower, conceiving his son? Isn't he busy for once?"

"She escaped."

"Of course, you had nothing to do with that." Celo shook his head and went back to his wood pile. "You've got to stop challenging him. It never ends well for you."

Venero ignored that bit of advice, just as he had a hundred times before. "She's coming this way, and you need to help her."

Celo turned, his eyes narrowed. "Of course, you had nothing to do with that either."

"Me?"

The youngest prince propped his hands on his knees and bent down so that his face was only a finger's breadth from Venero's toad face. "I don't need to do anything. And I'm *not* going to do anything that might attract his attention. I don't need that kind of trouble. Let her run through the forest until he finds her. Let them sort it out themselves."

"She needs help."

"She can ask her husband for some."

"She's very pretty."

Celo's eyes narrowed. "She's not my problem."

"I think she is." Venero lied, just a little. "That's why she's coming here."

Celo pushed a hand through his hair. He couldn't have looked less cooperative and his words were grudgingly uttered. "What do I have to do to get rid of her?"

"Stoke up your fire. She'll be wet and needs to get warm. Find some old clothes you can give her and heat up some soup. Then send her to the Queen's Grotto in the Citadel, as quickly as you can."

Celo flinched and took a step back. "I can't send

anyone to that place."

"I thought you wanted to get rid of her."

"But *there?* You know what Mother does to intruders."

"Which is why you need to give her your satchel, all packed with food for the journey."

"I don't understand."

Venero tried again to smile. "I'll be tucked inside."

Celo shook his head. "Who exactly needs to help her, Venero? You or me?"

"Me. But I have certain limitations at this time."

Consideration dawned in Celo's eyes. "What exactly is she to you? Are you hoping she'll help you?"

"She did already. That's why I can shield my thoughts and cast dreams again."

"She kissed you? When you're like that?" Celo was clearly astonished.

"No, she touched my forehead. It was enough to break part of the curse."

Celo chuckled. "Lost some of your charm?"

Venero found himself bristling. "I'm doing fairly well, considering the circumstances."

"But does that mean she's your true love?"

"There's no such thing as true love..."

"You'd better hope there is, unless you want to stay like that for the rest of your life."

Venero had nothing to say to that.

"A little awkward that she's married to Urbanus, isn't it?" Celo started to laugh then, which Venero thought entirely inappropriate.

"She's not my true love," he said with some annoyance. "But she's helpful, and I want to help her in return..."

"How?"

"Urbanus has cast a spell over her. She didn't deserve it. The antidote will be in the grotto."

Celo sobered. "Who ever deserves what they get in this kingdom?" He sighed. "All right. I'll help her, but don't be surprised if I do it quickly."

"I wouldn't be."

"And this is it. We're even forever now."

"Of course."

"And if Urbanus catches me—or Mother does—I'll say it was your fault." Celo dropped his voice. "I'll say you beguiled me into it. You admitted that your powers were back, after all."

Venero felt a grim resolve. "Deal."

Celo nodded and grabbed an armload of firewood. Venero hopped onto the top of the pile and his brother carried it to the hut. "That satchel," Celo said with a nod at a leather bag hanging from a peg. Venero jumped off the firewood, and Celo dumped it by the fire. He then put the bag on a bench and opened the flap. Venero hopped in and sighed, content that he could rest for a while.

"What happened to your leg?"

"It's cut and bruised. It hurts but it'll heal."

"How'd that happen?"

Venero grimaced. "She has a pavofel and it hunts."

"A pavofel?"

"Big mean bastard."

"A feline pet." Celo shook his head. "Just your luck. I know how you hate them. She *must* be pretty." Celo had taken down a crockery pot from the shelf above the table and crouched down beside the bench. He peeled back the protective covering and Venero smelled the pungent herbs in the unguent.

"She'll smell it."

"Chances are good she might need some, too. Or the pavofel."

"You're right. We jumped into the river to avoid spelldust. The pavofel wasn't amused."

Celo straightened as his expression turned to horror. "Spelldust? He loosed spelldust and you didn't tell me?"

"An unfortunate oversight. I told you now."

His brother exhaled and his lips tightened, but still he bent closer. "Let me see." Celo applied the unguent with a fingertip, and Venero sighed in relief as he felt its healing power warm his skin. "Just how pretty is she?" Celo murmured. "Beautiful?"

"She's a warrior princess from Incendium," Venero said, ducking the question.

"Of course, she is, but is she beautiful too?"

Venero sighed. "Yes. But a dragon shifter."

"You and your warrior women," Celo teased. "Maybe this form is doing you a favor. How long would it take her to fall in love with you otherwise?"

Venero didn't find the joke very funny. "I don't think we have to worry about that. She hates toads."

"Well, with any luck, you won't be one forever."

"Not luck, Celo. Planning."

"Right. Strategy." Celo met his gaze. "And using someone for your own purpose. Does she know where you're going to lead her?"

"Of course not."

"What would she think of your plan if you told her all of it?"

"It doesn't matter," Venero insisted. "It's reciprocal. She helps me and I help her. In the end, we both get what we want."

"Really?"

"This will serve the greater purpose..."

"Your greater purpose." Celo sighed and straightened. "Sometimes it's not that hard to believe that you and Urbanus are twins."

Venero was insulted, but he had to acknowledge the thread of truth in that. He wasn't being entirely fair to Gemma. If she'd still been able to become a dragon, he could have felt justified, but her resilience and beauty as a woman made him feel manipulative.

Maybe even unfair.

Which was why he didn't say anything more.

Gemma had lost track of time when she finally smelled the wood fire.

When she broke the surface of the stream under the shelter of a willow tree, its branches hanging over the stream like a bower, she smelled the fire. She was delighted at the sign that she might not be alone in this endless forest, but hesitated before emerging from the water.

Would the person who had lit the fire help or hinder her?

Would he (She? They?) just send her back to Urbanus, or somehow summon him to collect her?

Gemma paused, uncertain who to trust. This might be Urbanus' county or realm, and the people might be obliged to support his will.

There might be repercussions if they didn't.

Felice didn't share her caution. The pavofel wriggled and escaped her grip to leap to the bank. Felice shook thoroughly, scattering water in every direction, then fastidiously sniffed the air. She marched off, her wet tail waving like a bedraggled banner, and was so much her usual self that Gemma couldn't imagine the creature had been touched by spelldust. She hauled herself out of the river, wrung out the maid's dress as well as she could, shivered, sneezed, and followed Felice.

Smoke was rising from a tidy little hut, one that blended so well with the forest that Gemma might not have discovered it without the scent of the fire. A young man stood outside of it, gutting some fish, and Felice hastened forward to invite herself to a feast. He was fair-haired and tanned, dressed simply, yet tall and trim. His beard was long and his clothing was rustic but clean.

He started at the appearance of the pavofel, then smiled. "You're a long way from home, pavofel," he said, his voice quiet and pleasant. He cast a whole fish at Felice, who pounced upon it and set to devouring it. He lifted his gaze to Gemma then, and she had the definite sense that he wasn't surprised to see her. "Hungry?" he asked, and cleaned another fish.

"I am. Were you expecting company?" Gemma considered the number of fish he had caught and again imagined that her arrival had been anticipated.

"Your arrival is fortuitous," he said, not really answering her question. "I had so much luck fishing this morning that I couldn't stop." He shrugged and turned to the hut. "You've saved me the task of smoking them."

Was that an invitation?

If it was, should she accept?

The scent of the Seed teased Gemma's nostrils. "Is Urbanus here?" she asked.

The man started, his alarm clear. "No!" He stared at her for a moment, then appeared to be both relieved and amused. He disappeared into the hut, chuckling quietly, but left the door ajar. Felice finished her fish, then strutted toward the door, obviously in pursuit of more. Gemma smelled the fish roasting and her belly growled.

"Hurry up unless you like yours burned," he said from within the hut.

Gemma approached with caution. Why could she smell the Seed? She stood on the threshold, surveying the interior of the hut, then cast a long glance over the small clearing outside of it. All was still and it appeared that the man was her only companion. He was trying to hide a smile as he fed another fish to Felice.

"Do I amuse you?" Gemma asked. Arousal unfurled in her belly and sent a welcome heat through her. She swallowed, wondering how the Seed could be in this place.

"No, you remind me of someone. I won't harm you. Come in."

Gemma entered the cabin, more than ready to defend herself. Her host was only a little taller than her and slim. She suspected that he had a wiry strength that could be a surprise. Still, she thought she could best him in a fair fight.

"The question is whether there is ever a fair fight in Regalia," he said and she was startled. "Yes, I can read your thoughts, and yes, that's why I live alone in the wilderness. It is comparatively quiet here and I can think my own thoughts in peace."

"Comparatively?"

"The forests are full of creatures. Not all of them are spies." He offered her a ceramic plate, graced by a slice of bread and a grilled fish fillet. "Come sit by the fire and eat."

"Is that how you knew I was coming?"

He smiled and offered the plate again. She couldn't smell any guile in him and her sense was that he had no skill with deception.

Then she realized something. "How did you know what a pavofel was?"

"You knew what it was and I read your thoughts."

Gemma considered that as her belly grumbled. She chose to trust him, at least for the moment, and accepted his invitation. "Are you a prince of Regalia whose truth is hidden?"

He gave her a sharp glance. "If I was, I wouldn't be the one you're seeking."

But the Seed...

"He *was* here."

Her host said no more and Gemma ate before the fish got cold. Her thoughts churned all the while, her questions creating more questions, and the Seed making her yearn for satisfaction. The fire was warm and the fish was delicious. Gemma was certain she had never smelled or seen better fare at a feast.

Much less tasted it.

She ate three fish and felt much better. Felice was cleaning herself before the fire, her fur returning to its usual fluffy splendor.

Her host rose to his feet. "You should change your clothes and leave," he said so abruptly that Gemma was surprised.

"Do you often have visitors who you help and send on their way?"

"Almost never, thank goodness. I would rather you left sooner rather than later." His attention was snared by a bird call from outside the hut and his eyes narrowed as he listened. "You might be pursued." His manner made Gemma want to hurry.

Not all of the creatures in the forest were spies, by his own admission, but she'd bet that bird was.

He gestured to a pile of clothes and a satchel already packed. Gemma could see bread within it and smelled some herbal mixture. There also appeared to be a change of clothing. "Hurry! We'll talk as we go." He left the cabin then and she heard him make a bird call. A conversation ensured, or at least she imagined as much, for each time he gave a cry or a whistle, the bird in the trees seemed to respond. What news did the creature bring him?

Gemma dressed quickly. To her relief, he'd given her simple men's clothing: chausses, a chemise and vest, a belt and a pair of well-worn boots. She slung the satchel over her shoulder, wondering what to do with the maid's garments.

"Give them to me," he instructed, having reappeared in the doorway, and Gemma did. He doused the fire then and secured the door of the hut, then set off at a brisk pace. He walked in the same direction that the river flowed, but veered away from the water, taking a course that only he could discern through the forest.

"Where are we going?" Gemma asked.

"You're going to steal a mount from Farmer Aro. I'm just showing you the way." He spared her a glance. "I assume you can ride."

"Of course. Do you have any advice as to my direction?"

"You must go to the Queen's Grotto in the Citadel, in order to find the antidote you seek."

Gemma halted. "How do you know this?"

"A toad told me."

Gemma couldn't stop her smile. "It's alive, then? And you know it? Where is it?"

"It doesn't matter. It told me to expect you and what you needed."

"Why are you helping me?"

"Because I owe the toad a favor." He spoke with such solemnity that it had to be true.

This was a most peculiar realm.

Unless he'd known the toad before it had been cursed.

"Did you know him before he was cursed?" she asked and her companion flicked a warning look at her. "Will you tell me about it?"

The man sighed. He held back a cane of some plant that would have snapped in Gemma's face, then walked beside her instead of in front of her. "How much do you know about the royal family of Regalia?"

"Very little. The queen has twelve sons—well, eleven now." It seemed tactless to speak of Drakina's role in that, but her companion was unsurprised by the clarification.

He wasn't very interested in it either.

"Actually, it's commonly believed that the queen has

ten surviving sons, for one is missing. One also has retreated from her court and no longer enjoys her favor."

That would be Venero who was missing and assumed dead. Who was the son who had retreated?

Her companion winked at her.

Gemma smiled. It only seemed reasonable to her that sons of Queen Arcana might want to hide from their mother and her sorcery.

"Exactly," her companion agreed.

"So, she's down to nine."

"You could look at it that way. Do you know much about them?"

"Urbanus is crown prince, now that Canto is no more."

"And the missing prince?"

"Venero. He and Urbanus were twins. But not identical."

"Not at all. Venero's eyes were as gold as amber and it was said that his vision would burn through to the heart of any matter."

Gemma thought it was probably prudent to disguise how much she did know.

"Very prudent," agreed her companion. "But you know about the powers delegated to each son."

"What was Venero's power?"

"He was a DreamCaster. He could send dreams to others."

Gemma grimaced. "Like a MindBender."

"Similar but slightly different. Part of the distinction is nomenclature, but it's more than that. A MindBender can manipulate the thoughts of others. That's reliant upon the ability to read their minds. It's an innate ability."

"They're born with it?"

He nodded. "But it can be developed with training, too. Refined and expanded. Like the ability to do calculations in your mind. Someone has the talent but can make more of it."

"I understand."

"DreamCasting, though, is a given ability, granted by a sorcerer. It has specific limitations, as defined by the sorcerer who gave it, and usually, like most given magical abilities, a limitation."

"Like what?"

"Like a blind spot. There's some situations in which it doesn't work."

"Power tempered with vulnerability," Gemma mused.

"Exactly. So, Canto, as the son of the queen and the captain of the guard, had a natural talent for fighting. His magical ability was the power to win. That made him a champion, at jousts and tournaments."

"He didn't win against Drakina."

"She was his weak spot, the one individual he couldn't triumph against." Her companion trudged onward. "The queen is said to have confided this detail in him for the first time on the night before his wedding."

Which was why he'd stood up his bride.

"She wanted to clear the way for Urbanus?"

Her companion shrugged. "He was always a favorite."

"Who was his father?"

"A visiting wizard from Nimue. That's why his ability to cast spells is so strong. It's a combination of innate ability and a gift."

"And his weak spot?"

"I'll guess that the queen made him powerless against her, because that was Venero's weak spot."

Gemma nodded. "Who was his father?"

"A diplomat and lawyer from Advocia, part of the same delegation as Urbanus' father."

"How do you know that?"

"I peeked."

Gemma considered whose mind he must have peeked

into and had a good idea why he was hiding in the forest. Only the queen would have known that truth.

The other man remained silent and trudged onward.

"So, what happened to Venero?"

"No one knows," her companion said, although Gemma smelled that he lied. "He was a good man, a warrior who kept his word and treated others with honor."

'The opposite of Urbanus, then,' Gemma thought and her companion laughed.

"So, you *are* acquainted with the crown prince. I thought you might be."

Gemma endeavored to think nothing at all and was pretty sure she failed.

"You remind me of him, actually," the man said, halting before a line of scrub.

"Of Urbanus?"

"Of Venero. There's an integrity about you, and a clarity in your thinking." He nodded. "The way you assess situations and plan your reactions is much the same." He gave her a hard look. "You're not a sneak."

Gemma took that as a compliment. "Then maybe I would have liked *that* prince of Regalia."

"Maybe so. He had ideas to improve the situation of the people of Regalia and to diminish our reliance upon Incendium. People liked him."

Gemma guessed that Venero had to be removed because he might offer a challenge to Urbanus' taking the throne.

She wished he hadn't been.

"Careful what you wish for," her companion advised.

"I can wish for the goodwill of others, surely?"

"It's not more than that?"

Gemma shook her head with resolve. "It sounds like he might have made a good king, despite being a DreamCaster."

"The Consort of Incendium is a MindBender."

"And I distrust him, too. No one should mess with the thinking of anyone else."

"I'll take that under advisory." Her companion said mildly then paused. He pointed through the growth to a cluster of buildings. The barn was obvious, for there were goats penned beside it. The fields were tilled, the garden tended, and all looked tidy. "There is one swift horse, a black as midnight with a single star on his brow. He should be tethered in the last stall to the right."

"You want me to steal the horse?"

"It's too far to walk to the Citadel, especially if you're being pursued. You'll send it back."

Gemma nodded in understanding. "But how? There must be a dozen men working and who knows how many inside the barn."

"Farmer Aro and his men will go to the house for their midday meal at any moment now. They do it every day."

Even as he spoke, several men left the barn and walked toward the house, the low rumble of their conversation carrying to Gemma's ears.

"I guess three more," her companion said.

"Four," Gemma corrected. He spared her a glance prepared to argue. "I smell a fourth. Maybe he doesn't think much."

They waited, and three more men made their way to the house.

A moment later, just when Gemma thought her companion believed her to be wrong, another figure came out of the barn. He shuffled toward the house, moving more slowly than the others, and Gemma smiled at her companion's sidelong glance.

"Four," she whispered.

He nodded, then pointed. "Follow that road, the one that bends to the right. Take the right fork twice, and the road will lead you around the village. Eventually, it crosses a river and become a narrow track." He indicated the shadow of hills rising far to the right. "Its only destination after the river is the Citadel, and inside that palace, you'll find the Queen's Grotto. Let the horse go when you can see the watch tower. It will find its way home."

"Won't I need it to return?"

He spared her a look. "Either you will succeed and find the antidote you seek, or you'll die in the Citadel. Either way, you won't need the horse again."

He knew her true nature.

Of course.

"And the Seed?"

Her companion smiled. "You'll find it when the time is right."

Gemma eyed the mountains, seeing that the distance wasn't small. How many days would it take her to reach her destination? She would just have to make the best progress she could, and let the horse rest when necessary. She took a deep breath and nodded.

"I thank you for all of this," she said, turning toward her companion but he was gone, as surely as if he had never been there. "I hope he's not caught," she whispered, and something in her saddlebag moved.

"So do I," came the familiar voice of the toad. "But don't miss this chance. There might not be another."

CHAPTER FOUR

To Venero's pleasure, Gemma didn't waste time asking questions about his survival or his presence. She peeked into the satchel to confirm that he was there, smiled, then shut the flap again. His heart was skipping from just the glimpse of that triumphant smile. He felt her ease the satchel to her back and adjust her grip on the pavofel.

Then she ran, fast and low, loping smoothly across the field.

There was something to be said for a purposeful woman.

Even one who distrusted DreamCasters.

She stopped suddenly, pivoted, and must have backed against the barn because he was a little crushed. He made a tiny sound of protest.

"Sorry," she whispered, then was off again. He felt the shade of the building fall over her, then smelled the hay in the barn. The air was cooler and he knew she was inside. She moved silently and cautiously down the length of the barn, then caught her breath.

She wasn't moving.

There had to be a reason.

Venero climbed over the provisions and peeked out the side of the satchel, fearing that Celo had been wrong about the horse and its location. He hadn't been. The beast was there, watching Gemma, its coat as dark as midnight and the star on its brow glowing. It wore a bridle, which was tethered to the end of the stall, and its dark eyes seemed to be filled with wisdom.

"You beautiful creature," Gemma whispered, then stepped into the stall with her hand outstretched.

It was only when the horse stepped forward that Venero heard the rustle of its feathered wings.

"Hurry, hurry," he urged.

"I've never seen a pegasus," she replied quietly. "Besides, everyone knows that you have to take your time with a horse. They're not like Starpods."

"Hurry!" he urged, even though he knew she was right.

She put down the bag and the pavofel, which began to clean itself at a closer proximity than Venero would have liked. Gemma walked around the pegasus, running her hand over it, praising it quietly. Venero was so busy admiring the view of her that he forgot to anticipate her choice. She reached for the saddle that was at the end of the stall. Venero hadn't seen it there until she touched it.

"Not the saddle!" he hissed, but it was too late. The hundred silver bells upon it had already rung out a warning, erupting like a clarion as soon as Gemma's fingertips brushed against it. The pegasus stamped with impatience to run, and tossed its head, its wings flapping. Men shouted in the distance and footsteps could be heard running toward the barn.

"Thanks for the timely warning," Gemma muttered. She moved like lightning, even as she spoke.

"It's enchanted."

"Obviously." She had already slung the satchel over her shoulder again and untied the horse's bridle.

"You could have anticipated it."

He heard her grind her teeth.

"I don't understand magic. Since you seem to, you

might be a little more proactive in future."

"Hurry!" Venero urged but he was pretty sure it was too late.

Gemma seized the pavofel and stuffed it into the satchel, prompting Venero to recoil and the pavofel to hiss in protest.

"Deal with it," she muttered, leading the horse from the stall. She and the pegasus raced together to the doorway to the barn.

By the time Venero was able to peek out again, they were outside and a man was coming around the corner. Gemma kicked him hard in the gut, a nice high kick and beautifully executed. Venero had to admire her technique. The man fell to the ground with a groan, but there were three more behind him. Gemma was surrounded and separated from the pegasus, and the reins were tugged from her fingers.

But that was when she really set to work.

She decked one man, spun and drove her fingers into the eyes of one who was trying to snatch her from behind, then kicked the third in the crotch. She spun in place, so lethal and effective that Venero could have watched her all day. She was dressed in men's clothing, her hair braided back, but looked remarkably enticing. Even without her dragon, she was a force to be reckoned with. Venero tried to control his desire for his brother's wife and lost.

He averted his gaze from her, only to see that the pegasus was cantering away from the barn, gathering speed.

"It'll take flight without us!" he roared. He tried to cast a thought to the creature that it should slow down, and the pegasus slowed its pace only slightly.

Gemma spun and raced after the beast. She was faster than Venero expected, and more agile, too. She seized the tail of the pegasus and vaulted to its back with grace just as it took flight. Its hooves were above the ground and its dark wings beating hard. The satchel seemed to be floating behind Gemma, and Venero hoped the strap didn't snap. The reins were dangling out of reach, but Gemma knotted her hands into pegasus' dark mane. She looked back and laughed at the men left far below with a confidence Venero found both bold and attractive.

Before he could think too much about his changing notions about women, Gemma urged the pegasus to greater height and speed. The wind whistled past the satchel. The pavofel hissed, and Venero looked to see its eyes gleaming overhead. He yelped and tried to bury himself beneath the provisions, only to have the creature burrow after him.

"Help me!" he shouted.

"I'm busy," Gemma retorted. "Work it out between yourselves."

Her lack of sympathy was annoying. "I liked you better when you were trying to charm my brother," he muttered as he dodged the pavofel's paw. He tried to send a thought to the pavofel but it made no difference.

Maybe his restored powers were already ebbing away. That wasn't a reassuring thought!

"How so?" Gemma asked.

"Because you were demure." Even as he uttered the familiar words, Venero doubted their truth. He'd never found a woman as attractive as Gemma, and she was as different from his usual taste as possible.

And a dragon, too.

"Women should be demure, charming, and biddable," he insisted all the same. His reactions must be due to celibacy, which was unnatural. "It's more feminine."

"More feminine," Gemma echoed, with a precision that should have warned him.

Venero might have argued his case more eloquently if he hadn't been trying to evade the pavofel, which was, in fact, a very persistent hunter. He heard himself give a little squeak of fear that would have mortified him in his normal form, but it seemed to provoke Gemma to offer advice.

"You could do with some charm of your own," she noted.

"This is hardly the time to criticize..." The pavofel batted him to one side. Its claws were retracted, and he realized it was playing with him. He could still get hurt, but was slightly reassured that the beast didn't mean to consume him. Maybe she knew the creature better than he did.

Since it was her pet, that wasn't out of the question.

That hardly improved his mood.

"She likes being rubbed on the stomach," Gemma said, a tinge of impatience in her tone. "Right where the blue blends to green. Maybe you could manage to make friends while I'm busy saving our lives."

Make friends. With a pavofel.

Or really, with any creature intent upon injuring him.

While Gemma saved their lives. Venero hated that he had to admit his reliance upon his companion. He was a prince! He was supposed to save damsels in distress.

But Gemma was doing just fine on her own.

"I hate pavofels."

"So you've said. What do you have against them?" Gemma chuckled. "They're beautiful and charming, and Felice is female."

Venero would have liked to glare at her. "They hunt."

"Rather well, too."

"Warrior or beauty, not both."

"I'll keep that in mind," Gemma said, as if she might be mocking him.

Felice gave a little growl and moved her paw closer. Venero met the pavofel's brilliant gaze and swallowed his pride. Desperate times called for desperate means. He would be trapped in this bag with this creature for a while.

Venero crept closer to Felice's heat, well aware that he risked everything in the approach. He eased up against her belly, she hissed, but he stretched out a leg and rubbed.

Right where the blue blended to green.

The pavofel adjusted its position and Venero feared the worst. He retreated but Felice yowled softly, as if in invitation.

She was just giving him better access to its stomach. She was making demands of him. Venero moved closer and rubbed again, as the pavofel lounged contentedly over the provisions.

Venero rubbed in a gentle rhythm, right where the blue fur changed to green. It was far less than what he wanted to contribute to their success, but there wasn't much else he could do.

Felice stretched, yawned, closed her eyes, and began to purr.

Not feminine.

Gemma would let that comment pass for the moment, but she certainly wouldn't forget it. She was doing all the work and taking all the risks, and the toad was criticizing her! If she hadn't suspected that she needed his knowledge of Regalia to succeed in capturing the antidote, she might have tipped him right out of the satchel and let him fall.

No. She wasn't mean. She'd wait until they landed and *then* tip him out of the bag.

Warrior or beauty, not both.

That burned. How dare he imagine that because she was attractive, she couldn't be effective, too? She could have simpered and fluttered her eyelashes at those men on the farm, and they wouldn't be soaring across the sky on the pegasus. She was taking him where he wanted to go, but he wasn't giving her any credit for that.

Maybe she didn't need the toad badly enough to put up with his comments. She'd managed to find shelter and a meal by herself, after all, as well as provisions and directions to the Citadel. He wasn't quick to admit his secrets, that was for sure.

Could his objective be different than he'd admitted?

Could he be using her for his own purposes, whatever they might be?

Could he be encouraging her to leap from the fat to the fire?

Gemma didn't know and she didn't like it. She wished she had the power of the bearded man in the hut to read the thoughts of others. Then she'd know for sure what the toad had planned.

After the initial thrill of taking flight with the pegasus—which made her feel like her old self again, and increased her determination to get her shifter powers back—she'd been wondering. She'd been told to send the horse back when she saw the watch tower. But if she could see the watch tower, surely those guards in the watch tower would be able to see her? She had to think that a black pegasus would be hard to miss.

She shook the satchel. "How will I know when we're getting close?" she asked. "I want to send the pegasus back before there's any chance of it being seen."

"Are you following the road?" the toad asked.

"Of course." She refrained from rolling her eyes. Maybe being logical or following instructions weren't feminine traits either, according to this toad. Maybe he'd rather be lost.

Maybe she could help with that.

"What's beneath us now?"

"Tilled fields. To the far left, there's a town. It's pretty far away, but something is glinting in the sun.

Maybe the spire of a metal tower. It looks as if there are a lot of buildings clustered together there."

"That would be a town, then," the toad commented. "Well done."

"Are you always so cranky?"

"Only when I'm trapped in a bag with a predator that wants to eat me when I'm unable to do much about it."

"Rub the spot..."

"I know, I know! Can't you hear the noise this thing is making?"

Gemma smiled. Felice was purring louder than she had in a while. "You must be doing it right."

"My life is reduced to finding the right spot to rub on a pavofel's belly."

"As opposed to being at the nexus of politics and diplomacy, where a toad rightfully belongs?" Gemma asked, then caught herself. "Actually, on this planet, that might be exactly where a talking toad belongs." She wondered again who he really was.

Not everyone was taught Latin, after all.

She surveyed the land before them. "There are foothills rising in the distance."

"And a broad river flowing before them. "

"Have you been here before?"

The toad seemed to hesitate before replying. "Someone brought me here once," he admitted, and Gemma sensed a half-truth.

"You're pretty well traveled for a toad."

"I told you: I wasn't always a toad."

"But of course, you won't actually tell me anything about yourself, because you never do."

"Maybe I can't," he retorted with some annoyance.

Maybe. If he was trying to win her sympathy and interest, he'd lost it with 'not feminine.' "Looks like a mill to the right, and maybe a village."

"Go left," the toad said sharply. "There's a spur that

comes down from the foothills."

"I see it! It's heavily forested, so we'll fly lower and maybe not be seen."

"That would be better."

Gemma thought she detected sarcasm in his tone. She bit back a retort because she still needed his help. "So, the Citadel is at the end of the road, and this spur will hide us from view?"

"You know that."

She allowed her own tone to become irritable. "But what I don't know is how we get to the Citadel without being seen, even on foot."

"There's a tunnel. Of course."

"Under the spur of the mountain."

"Exactly."

"Well, won't anyone guarding the Citadel be guarding the tunnel, too?"

"Of course, but that doesn't mean it's a bad way in."

Another half-answer. Gemma sighed and frowned. "I suppose you'll only tell me more when you think the time is right."

"Information is valuable. If I told you everything right now, you might not take me with you."

"Because you're such delightful company."

He didn't reply to that.

Gemma guided the pegasus far to the left and urged it to fly close to the ground. There was a coniferous forest with very old growth that spread from the flanks of the mountain spur and across the land to that broad river. She rode up the side of the spur until the trees thinned, then tugged on the mane of the pegasus. It landed elegantly and shook its head, lingering only long enough for her to slip from its back and kiss the star on its brow in gratitude. Then it took flight again and turned back, heading for the warmth of a familiar stable.

Gemma shaded her eyes to watch it fly, admiring its

grace and beauty.

At least she did until her satchel squirmed. She opened the top and Felice leaped out. The pavofel shook itself, then sat down on the path. Its tail swished.

"Peace at last," the toad muttered.

Gemma ignored that comment. She slung the bag over her shoulder and surveyed the side of the mountain. "Are you going to give me any hints, or do I have to find the tunnel entrance myself?"

The flap of the satchel was nudged open and she saw the nose of the toad. "It's up there," he said, and she supposed he was pointing with his injured foot. "There was a little track that came out of the last of the forest, probably used by goatherds and their flocks."

"Was," Gemma echoed. She strode through the forest, eyes on the ground. "How long ago were you here?"

"It doesn't matter. The track will still be there."

"Who brought you here?"

"It doesn't matter."

"What happened to the person who brought you here?"

"That really doesn't matter."

Gemma found the track and halted. "What if I say it does?"

"That doesn't matter either."

Gemma swung the satchel around and opened it, peering down at the toad. "I don't know who you think you are or who you were, but you're cranky, you're bossy, and you're a lot of trouble. I don't know for sure that you're on my side, and I'm not going into the Queen's Grotto in the Citadel without being sure that I can trust whoever goes in there with me." She gave him a determined look. "I need to know more about you."

"I liked you a lot better when you were trying to charm Urbanus."

"So you said. What's that supposed to mean?"

"I thought for a moment that Urbanus had made a good choice of bride..."

Gemma bristled that this toad expressed any admiration for Urbanus who had, after all, drugged her on their wedding night. "Then why did you befriend me to take you to the Citadel?"

"Desperation, plain and simple." The toad seemed to wince. "When you wait for opportunity as long as I have, you have to make the most of whatever comes along."

"Even a warrior who isn't feminine?"

"Even..." he began but Gemma had heard enough.

She didn't need his help nearly so badly as he thought she did. She reached into the bag, picked up the toad and lifted him until she was looking him in the eye. He seemed to almost be smiling, and she had the sense he was quite satisfied with his situation.

"This is much better than that bag," he began, but Gemma didn't let him finish.

"Too bad then that you didn't take your own advice." She could have flung him down, but she didn't like to hurt any creature unnecessarily. Instead, she put him down on the track and turned away. Felice looked between her and the toad, ears flicking.

"What advice?" he croaked and took a hop toward her.

"To make the most of whatever comes along. Insulting me is a pretty bad choice when you need my help." Gemma waved. "See you in the Citadel, maybe." She turned to walk briskly up the mountain track, knowing he'd never be able to catch up with her. Felice loped along behind her, matching her pace.

"Hey!" the toad shouted and she heard him hopping behind her. "Hey! You *need* my help!"

"Not badly enough to listen to you," she retorted, striding on. "And if you need *me*, your manners could use some improvement." She paused and looked back, barely able to discern him far behind her. "How's this for demure?"

She didn't wait for a reply, just hiked more quickly up the side of the mountain, seeking the entry to the tunnel. Anger gave her energy and she covered ground quickly. The sky was getting darker and it would be good to find shelter before night fell. Gemma couldn't begin to imagine what might lurk in the wilderness of Regalia.

She felt a twinge of guilt about the toad, left to defend himself in the wilderness, but refused to turn back for him.

Demure. That word alone was enough to make her growl.

Venero had to admit that speaking his mind at this particular juncture might not have been the smartest choice.

But he'd been under duress.

Trapped with a pavofel.

Enchanted as a toad.

Powerless to affect his own fate.

Reliant upon his brother's wife.

Who pretty much defied his every notion of what a woman should be like, and yet, *and yet*, was remarkably attractive. Troublingly so, in fact. Venero couldn't understand it, and that irked him most of all. She was a dragon shifter—well, she would be again, if she got the antidote—and she fought like Arista. She was decisive and blunt and still incredibly beautiful. She challenged his assumptions and made him glad, in a strange way, that he was cursed to be a toad, so he couldn't make an inappropriate advance.

Never mind that he was willingly returning to the site where everything had gone wrong in the first place. It was only natural to feel some concern in venturing close to his mother's sanctuary—where he'd been caught in league with a traitor to the crown and had paid the price.

Venero knew he had to accompany Gemma to Queen's Grotto in the Citadel for the sake of the greater good, but he didn't have to like it.

He hopped after Gemma and admitting that traveling with her was a lot easier than journeying alone, even accounting for the pavofel.

At least he knew where she was going. He could find the tunnel entrance, and suspected she would as well. She seemed to be quite competent, which was a good trait in a comrade.

It might even be a good trait in a romantic partner, if he was going to need to outrun his mother and brother for the foreseeable future.

She had also given him some of his powers back, with a touch of a fingertip. Even if they were still compromised, that was better than nothing at all.

The conclusion from that was obvious and unwelcome. It defied everything Venero believed that a woman like Gemma could be his true love.

He didn't even believe in true love.

He sighed and hopped, considering the merit of trying to cast Gemma a dream. It seemed like a bad idea, given her prejudice against MindBenders.

He sensed that such a course of action could go badly awry.

But Gemma would need his advice to survive the Grotto and he needed her help to break his own curse. They needed each other—but more importantly, Venero knew that he owed her an apology.

Never mind that Gemma might perish, because he'd led her this far and she didn't know—she couldn't know—what was ahead.

Venero had to catch up and make this right.

The cave entrance wasn't immediately obvious, but Gemma finally found it just as the sun was sinking. It was a good thing, actually, that it was hard to find, as that meant it was less likely she'd be pursued.

Well, except by the toad.

She climbed the side of the mountain instead of following the long switchbacks of the path, wanting to reach shelter before darkness fell completely. Felice jumped ahead of her and finally, the darkness of an opening loomed before them. Her hands were scratched and her feet were sore. She glanced down at the long route she'd traveled and wondered, just a little, what had happened to the toad.

If he wasn't smart enough to cultivate alliances where necessary, she decided she shouldn't worry about him.

Even if she did.

Gemma crouched at the threshold of the cave and opened the satchel. To her relief, there were a couple of candles and a flint. She took one and lit it, then hoisted the satchel and entered the cave with caution. There was only silence from within, but without knowing its depth and dimensions, she couldn't be sure she and Felice were alone.

If nothing else, this might be the cave that led to the tunnel that led to the Citadel, and if so, it would be guarded at some point.

The candlelight illuminated a space that was more like a hollow etched out of the side of the mountain. It wasn't very deep, and wouldn't offer much protection if the wind turned. Felice sauntered toward the back corner with a confidence about the cave that Gemma didn't share, then disappeared. The pavofel mewed and the sound echoed.

Gemma followed, only to discover that there was an opening in that back corner. It was only a narrow slit, but the shadows from the rocks surrounding it had disguised it from view. She peered through it, then surveyed the short and low corridor beyond. Once she stepped through, she could barely stand upright. There was a stream running in a crack in the floor along the length of the tunnel and it sloped upward.

Maybe it wasn't the tunnel to the Citadel.

Felice was marching onward, her tail high.

Gemma looked left and right, then hugged her satchel closer and followed. The tunnel turned twice then terminated with a small and low hole. The water bubbled through this hole, that crevice carved in the bottom of the opening as well. Felice, who usually disliked water, continued through the hole. The diameter of the hole was big enough that the pavofel didn't even have to lower her tail.

Gemma hesitated only a moment, then dropped to her hands and knees. It was difficult to carry the candle when she had to crawl through the gap—never mind avoiding the water that flowed down the middle—but she managed it.

When she stood up in the chamber beyond, she caught her breath in astonishment at the sight before her eyes.

She stood in a natural chamber shaped like a hemisphere. The highest point was probably twice her height and the walls were quite smooth. The rock looked to be a pinkish-gold in the light of her candle, with glimmers of crystal embedded in the stone. A pool had formed at one end of the chamber, and it emanated a refreshing chill. The water splashed a little, because it flowed down that back wall and into the pool. Beyond the pool was another narrow slit, probably offering access to more tunnels and caves.

But the remarkable thing was that the walls were adorned with the designs the Warrior Maidens of Cumae drew when they meditated in preparation for battle.

Gemma had participated in the ritual many times while in training on that planet. She remembered the cleansing of the body, the bathing and removal of hair. She remembered the mixing of pigments, the grinding of roots and herbs, and the blending of that with oil to create the familiar russet hue that embellished these walls. She remembered the painting of the body with protective symbols, the camaraderie of adorning another warrior with such talismans where she couldn't reach to do it herself. They'd stood in a circle, each painting the back of another, humming the music of war. She remembered the communal meal, the prayer, and the adornment of the walls of the caves.

Those from other civilizations thought the ritual was an invocation to the gods, but the Cumaens didn't believe in deities. They saw the sequence as a meditative exercise, one that would both focus the will of the individual warrior and build a sense of union between members of the company. That, in their view, was a better indication of success.

On Cumae, the caves had been painted many, many times, and Gemma had always felt a connection with past warriors as she drew her lines over theirs. This cave had been painted once, with deliberation and skill. The whorls and circular designs were a band of power on the walls, spilling into each other, feeding each other, flowing all around the room. They seemed to draw together disparate elements and stray power, then drive it all to the final culmination point. Gemma turned in place, remembering the surge of energy that she'd always felt when the last painted line connected with the first, making the circle complete.

It was similar to the jolt of the last line connected the images of the body paint into a coherent whole.

Where the end and the beginning connected on the cave walls, there was always a medallion, and this one was no different. The circular mark was always lavishly decorated, as befit a focus of power. The Warrior Maidens participating in the ritual, preparing for war, always signed the medallion with their own marks as their last deed before battle.

There was only one mark on this medallion, and Gemma's heart stuck in her throat as she stood before it and traced the familiar insignia with a fingertip.

Arista.

Gemma blinked back her tears. Arista had been on Regalia. She had been in this cave. She had painted all of this herself. She had departed from this cave to fight for some cause or another. She had won, because she had returned to Cumae, only to be killed.

Arista's time on Regalia must be at least part of the reason Urbanus had paid for her assassination. Why had she been here? She had gone into a battle of some kind, given that she'd painted this cave.

Had she survived alone with no one to paint her back?

Or had she fought with a companion?

Who?

Gemma's heart clenched at the notion of Arista taking another Sword Sister. But there was only one signature in the medallion, only Arista's own. If she'd fought with another, that person hadn't been trained on Cumae.

Which was very strange. The Warrior Maidens of Cumae trusted only their own kind. Arista must have fought alone.

Why had Arista been on Regalia?

What had she done?

That seemed, actually, like a good question to ask the toad, and once again, Gemma regretted leaving him behind. She would have to venture into the Queen's Grotto alone, without his advice, and find the antidote to her spell, without any idea what it might look like or where it might be. She was entering battle with less than perfect preparation. She sensed that Arista's story was an important detail, and she didn't know much about the queen's powers, either.

Maybe Gemma had been a little impetuous.

But what was done was done. She could go back for the toad, but didn't imagine it would be easy to find him. He would have left the path for his own protection, and with the coloring of his skin, she'd never see him.

Especially at night.

Maybe she should take advantage of this unexpected gift and prepare herself for the uncertainties ahead in the way she knew best.

Gemma wasn't superstitious but in this cave, in this moment, she felt as if Arista's ghost was right beside her. It made no sense, until she brushed her fingertips over her Sword Sister's familiar signature one more time and loosed a stone.

The wall had been patched, quickly, and the marks disguised the spot.

Gemma pulled her knife and dug at the crumbling surface. She caught her breath when a small metal capsule glinted in the light, then fell and rolled across the cavern floor. She pursued it and picked it up, smiling as she examined it in the light. It was about the size of her thumbnail, spherical, and smooth.

It was a Cumaen *memoria*.

Some part of Arista was in the palm of Gemma's hand.

Maybe Gemma wouldn't arrive at the Citadel as unprepared as she'd feared.

A Cumaen *memoria* was a one-time recording device used by the Warrior Maidens as a secure means of passing intelligence to those who followed. The manufacture of the device was a closely guarded secret, requiring no less than twenty-seven separate steps, each of which was understood by only a single individual on Cumae at any given time. The identities of the Twenty-Seven were so secret that each of them knew the identity of only one other, the one to whom he or she delivered the device after completing the assigned phase. The coordination of the manufacture of each *memoria* was managed by the computer known as the Hive, built in the depths of the Vaults of Cumae.

Gemma hadn't seen one since she'd left her training. The individual *memoria* were indistinguishable from each other. Although the surface of the *memoria* appeared to have no sensors or seams, it responded to an oral command, set by the owner. The device recognized only the code word uttered by the owner, and the same word uttered aloud by the owner's Sword Sister. Sword Sisters were forbidden to reveal a code word, under penalty of death, and not a one by the time Gemma left Cumae had ever divulged such a code, even under torture.

Betrayal of one's fellows was a greater indignity than any pain that could be inflicted upon the body. They were taught that, and those who could not uphold this duty were discharged from training.

Given where she had found the *memoria*, Gemma could only assume it had been programmed by Arista. She held it in the palms of her hands for a long moment, then bent and whispered Arista's code word to the device.

For a long moment, nothing happened. Gemma wondered whether Arista had chosen another code word, or taken another Sword Sister, then the *memoria* began to hum on her palm. It vibrated, then a seam was revealed and it split in half like an egg. The interior projector unfolded itself and a beam of light was projected across the cavern.

A hologram.

Of Arista.

Gemma sat down hard at the sight. She was amazed by how real her friend appeared to be. Arista was crouched before her, dressed for war, her hair shorter than it had ever been. The blue tattoo on her neck seemed darker, as if her tan had faded, but the gleam of purpose in her dark eyes was just the same.

"I don't know why I'm recording this," she confessed, her husky voice making Gemma ache with its familiarity. She spoke crisply and without hesitation, not wasting a gesture. "Only my Sword Sister can ever view it, and I can't imagine any circumstance that would ever bring Gemma to this cave. But I am confronted by such a puzzle that I wish I had a dragon's ability to solve a riddle, especially one that seems to have no good solution."

Felice looked up at the sound of Arista's voice. The blue hair bristled on the back of her neck and she stalked the hologram, eyes shining.

Arista looked directly at her, and Gemma's breath caught that her friend seemed to be looking straight into her eyes. "Maybe Gemma will sense my appeal, and her abilities will help me." Arista shook her head. "That sounds more like the magic and whimsy of the Regalians than anything that has ever crossed my lips. This is a curious place, to be sure, and there is no telling what has been influencing my thoughts, even without my awareness. I have, after all, been traveling in the company of a DreamCaster."

Had Venero been with Arista? Or was that ability common on Regalia?

Felice pounced on the hologram and passed right through it. The pavofel rolled and rose to her feet, spinning to assault the image again.

Arista sighed and pushed to her feet, pacing across

the chamber. The pavofel darted between the display of her legs, then retreated to the perimeter of the cave. Just before Arista pivoted, her image faded, perhaps because she had stepped beyond the range of the projector. Felice crouched to watch the hologram, ears folded back against her head. Arista returned to her former position and folded her arms across her chest, staring at the device.

"To review: I came to Regalia on a mission. The assignment was said to have come from the queen herself, although there is (naturally) no official confirmation of that. My task was to eliminate Prince Venero, the third son born to Queen Arcana—although there is some debate as to which twin was born first, the queen herself counts Urbanus as second and Venero as third. The fee was quite high, there being a considerable risk in eliminating one of the royal family. It was understood that I might not manage to leave Regalia after completing my mission, and that if I was captured, no one would come to my aid, not even the queen. I wonder if it was to look as if someone on Incendium was behind the assassination." Arista smiled thinly. "Even Cumae would disavow any knowledge of my presence on Regalia, and I would be considered a rogue."

Gemma was startled that Arista would have agreed to any assignment that might have left a stain on her reputation. What had the second mission been?

CHAPTER FIVE

Arista's hologram continued. "I agreed to the terms because I had another incomplete assignment that led to Regalia: this mission would serve as suitable cover. I had been charged to retrieve a valuable relic that was rumored to have been stolen by Queen Arcana. I was to bring it back to Cumae. I came to Regalia alone, so that no other lives would be risked."

Gemma could easily believe that Arista would sacrifice her own life to fulfill an assignment for Cumae.

Arista shook her head. "I didn't believe in sorcery before I came to Regalia, and I'm still not certain that magic is the cause for my current situation. But the fact remains that this quest has been very strange, and coincidence is a poor explanation for what transpired. I arrived on Regalia under the cover of being a diplomat, sent to negotiate updated terms for the Galactic Trade Alliance. I sought out Prince Venero at the palace soon after my arrival, for he was said to offer counsel to the queen on matters of diplomacy and law."

She smiled. "I expected him to be easy to kill, a nobleman convinced of his own safety and one accustomed to indulging his every whim, without regard for others. I expected to feel no qualms." Arista frowned. "It was not his good looks that swayed me, nor even the splendor of his body. He indulged in humor, which I did not always understand and for this, he mocked me. I recalled your counsel, Gemma, that such mockery could be done in affection, and was known as teasing, so I endured it with apparent good humor." Arista shook her head. "I did not expect him to surprise me, but he did. Venero not only acknowledged the existence of the prize I sought but said he knew its location. He proposed to be my ally and aid me in its retrieval from the treasury in the Queen's Grotto."

Gemma was fascinated.

Arista shrugged. "Why would a prince betray his mother and his kingdom? Perhaps because he knew my other assignment and where it had originated. But the fact was that I had need of someone who understood Regalia better than me." Arista fell silent and Gemma wondered how much more hologram the *memoria* could contain.

"I calculated the odds of my success alone to be much lower than those with Venero, even if he proved to be untrustworthy in the end. And so I accepted his proposition."

Arista looked up, her expression so anguished that Gemma reached out a hand to console her, forgetting she viewed a mere hologram. "He surprised me yet again, for I fell in love with him."

Gemma gasped. That Arista should fall in love was astonishing. Had she been enchanted? She wondered more about Prince Venero and his ability to DreamCast. Had he convinced Arista of something that wasn't true?

"I never expected this to happen to me. I do not know what to do." Arista began to pace, her concern clear. "Should I kill him and fulfill my assignment, even knowing that I will never forgive myself for destroying my love? Should I let him live until I retrieve the treasure from the queen, if indeed she truly possesses it? Should I betray him? Should I trust him fully? Should I tell him how I feel, offer myself, and create an alliance with him? The honor is greatest with the first option, but I confess to you alone that the last option has the greatest appeal."

She frowned and shook her head. "What manner of mother would hire an assassin to eliminate one of her sons? And why? There is more to this tale than I have gleaned, and Venero, I suspect, learned young to be wary of others. He guards his secrets close and his trust is elusive." Arista lifted her gaze and once again, Gemma felt that her Sword Sister was truly before her. "Could it be the love truly does conquer all?"

Gemma reached out with her free hand, but the hologram sputtered. The image disappeared, and the device whirred as it locked itself once more. Gemma closed her hand over it, feeling the warmth of the metal and wondered at what she'd seen. As much as she wished to watch the hologram again, she knew the *memoria* was spent or close to it. It wouldn't display the entire recording without being recharged. That might be possible, but only on Cumae. She closed her eyes and recalled Arista's confession, her memory training under that same warrior's instruction coming to her aid.

The Queen's Grotto was a treasury.

Was the prize Arista sought still there?

Or had she escaped with it? If she had, that might explain the choice of Urbanus. Had the assassin retrieved the treasure for Queen Arcana? Or had Arista hidden it? It was a bit late to think she should have asked more questions of Drakina's husband, Troy, about Arista's demise.

Felice trotted to her side, then twined around her ankles. Gemma picked up Arista's last gift to her and hugged the creature close. Felice began to purr.

Had Arista killed the man she loved?

Or had she taken Venero back to Cumae with her? Gemma straightened. If Venero had escaped Regalia, that would explain his disappearance—and it might also explain the subsequent assassination of Arista. Whether she had taken the prince captive, spirited him away with his consent or killed him, Arcana or Urbanus could have decreed that she had committed a crime on Regalia.

Never mind the relic or treasure.

How did any of this tale influence Gemma's own situation? She was here to avenge Arista, but how much did Urbanus know of her scheme? Arista's assertion that Venero had known her secret quest was troubling. Gemma thought of the birds flying overhead, and the claim of the bearded man that the woodland creatures could be spies. She thought of his ability to read her thoughts and wondered how hidden she and her objectives could possibly be.

She felt vulnerable, which she detested. She had to do something to improve her situation. Gemma put the *memoria* into her satchel, hiding it in an interior pocket. Felice rubbed against the satchel, but there was nothing within it that the pavofel would eat. Still, Gemma offered the pavofel some bread, but Felice turned up her nose and stalked away, presumably to hunt.

Arista's recording had given Gemma more questions than answers, but she felt empowered by seeing her Sword Sister. It had been good to hear her voice again. She turned to watch Felice, who crouched in the opening that led back to the path up the mountain, watching something.

Gemma smiled.

The ability of a dragon to solve a riddle. Yes, Arista had always said that was Gemma's gift. Could she solve this one?

The ritual Arista had taught her might help to clear her confusion and focus her thoughts. Gemma stood and shed her clothing quickly, then washed in the pool of water. The small cup of dye left in one corner gave her purpose. She would prepare herself for battle, in the way she had been taught on Cumae, and hope that the familiarity of the ritual would help her find the answers she needed.

Venero had never hopped so long or so hard as he had in recent days. If this alliance didn't succeed, it might just kill him. He was exhausted and sore by the time he made the sanctuary of the cave. He was panting when the shadow closed over him, but he didn't stop there. There was no sign of Gemma, but he could smell her skin. She would have explored, and he wondered how far she had ventured.

There was no sign of the pavofel either, which was a relief.

He could hear a woman's voice, and in his state of concern, it sounded like Arista. That made no sense, but he followed the sound anyway. Perhaps the stone was distorting the sound of Gemma's voice.

Venero went through the crack to the tunnel, then hopped its length to the small hole. He could see the warm glow of a candle's light through that hole, which encouraged him and gave him new strength.

He'd have a drink of water there.

It seemed to take forever to journey the length of the tunnel. Venero finally emerged from the other end of the tunnel that he'd once crawled through on his hands and knees, he halted to stare.

Gemma was humming.

More importantly, Gemma was nude.

Surprise weakened his knees, but as a toad, Venero didn't have far to fall. He stared and pretty much forgot everything except his desire.

Gemma was painting the walls of the grotto, following the lines that Arista had made. He recalled Arista performing the same ritual. Even as a son raised in a household brimming with sorcery, he'd been skeptical. There was no incantation. There was no sacrifice. There had been no talismans or tokens. How could this ritual accomplish anything?

But he'd felt the effectiveness of it at the end. He'd almost seen the power swirl around the perimeter and then around Arista after she'd made her mark. He'd seen her straighten and had seen the gleam of purpose in her eyes when she turned to consider him.

Oh, it had worked. Arista had been so intent upon her goal that she might have had only one purpose. She would have killed him without hesitation, if she'd perceived him as a threat to her quest.

And that was when he'd realized why he couldn't send her dreams.

Arista didn't have any.

He'd wanted to run but knew she would guess why. Instead, he held his ground and kept his expression the same. He'd ensured that his breathing was at the same rate and tried to control his pulse.

She'd sensed that, of course. She'd been designed to note every detail, as all androids were.

But she'd attributed his quickened pulse to the wrong cause.

He didn't want to think about Arista turning toward him, an invitation in her eyes.

Or his rejection of her advances.

Or his belated fear that he'd made a foolish choice.

Instead, he watched Gemma, an entirely different reaction coursing through him this time. She was as powerful a warrior as Arista had been, but possessed of a feminine beauty that fascinated him. Her charm had caught his interest, but it was her persistence that intrigued him—against every expectation, Venero desired a warrior woman.

This one.

He was so busy admiring Gemma that it took him a long time to realize that she echoed the sweep of the symbols with the same fluid grace as Arista.

His heart sank.

She *knew* these symbols.

She knew this ritual.

She *had* trained on Cumae. It wasn't just propaganda. That was why she'd fought so well when stealing the pegasus. That was why she knew how to ride and could vault into a saddle. That was why she'd examined the wedding chamber with such purpose.

Did she have more than training in common with Arista?

Venero didn't want to consider that, but he had to face the possibility.

No, he had to eliminate it.

Gemma paused before the circular medallion that Arista had painted last. She traced the outline of the circle and the marks that embellished its circumference. What was in the paint? Wine? Blood? It stained the old marks red, renewing and strengthening them, and Venero felt that same power rising.

She meant to go to battle, just as Arista had.

That was when he noticed the hole where the middle of the medallion should have been and wondered at it, remembering how he'd come upon Arista smoothing a paste over that very mark. He'd thought that she had been painting the stone for the placement of the medallion, but maybe she'd been doing more than that. Had she hidden something in the wall of the cavern and marked the spot with the medallion?

As he watched, Gemma pricked her finger and traced Arista's mark with her own blood. Her movements were confident.

She even knew Arista's mark.

Had he heard Arista's voice?

Either way, he knew that Gemma had married Urbanus for a very specific reason and it wasn't because she was stupid. He took a little hop closer in his concern and inadvertently kicked a pebble.

Gemma spun and crouched at the sound, prepared to defend herself. Her eyes glittered and he feared for a moment that she would shift shape to her dragon form.

In the same instant he recalled she couldn't do that anymore, she saw him and she eased her pose.

Venero could only stare in wonder. His heart skipped at the full sight of her beauty. The light of the candle seemed to caress her skin, turning her to gold. Her hair was loose and long, like spun sunlight, and her eyes glowed. She was radiant, as if illuminated from within.

He would have given anything in that moment to have been a man again, to have had Gemma's features light at the sight of him.

He certainly wouldn't have declined anything she offered.

No matter what the cost.

And that should have been a more terrifying notion than it was.

"You made it!" Gemma declared, and she bent down to peer at him, laughing with pleasure that made his heart clench.

The pavofel pounced then, appearing out of the shadows. Venero cried out as it caught him between his paws, then gave him a shake.

"Felice!" Gemma cried, picking the beast up by the scruff of its neck. She shook it hard and the pavofel released its grip. Venero fell to the hard ground, winced, then hopped to hide under the satchel. He saw the feet of the creature as it paced around the bag, and hunkered low.

"You knew Arista," he said, knowing he sounded cranky again.

Gemma didn't reply.

Venero moved to peek out from beneath the bag, wanting to see her reaction. "You know her name. You know she made these marks. You know *her* mark."

Gemma cast him a glance before she nodded acknowledgment. "And *you* knew what a pavofel was."

He had slipped up. "Maybe I read more than the maid."

"Maybe you learned about them from Arista. They're indigenous to Cumae, and their breeding is carefully managed there."

"Guilty as charged," Venero admitted.

"She was the one who brought you here."

Venero nodded, because it was more or less true. Actually, he had led Arista to this place, but he'd still been a man then. It had been part of their bargain.

"Were you going to help her kill Venero or get the relic from the Queen's Grotto?"

"The relic."

"Why not the prince?"

Venero hesitated. "I liked him."

"I heard he was popular," Gemma noted.

Venero quickly changed the subject. "Did I hear Arista's voice again?"

Gemma smiled. "What do you think?"

"That there was something embedded in the rock there, where that hole is now, something she hid for someone else. That you found it or maybe were looking for it all along."

"I didn't know about it before I found it."

"And you listened to a recording left by her."

Gemma nodded. "You're right, but the *memoria* wasn't left for just anyone."

"I don't understand." Arista had known Gemma would follow her? What was a *memoria?*

"A *memoria* can only be opened by the owner or the

owner's Sword Sister."

Venero fought the urge to retreat. He didn't like the sound of this. "Sword Sister?"

Gemma crouched down, her eyes bright. "She taught me and then we trained together. We painted each other's backs. We relied completely upon each other, and so we swore to be Sword Sisters." Gemma's expression was filled with resolve. Again, Venero had the sense that he faced an android, programmed for only one purpose. A warrior who could not be swayed or stopped.

A dragon and an android? It couldn't be. He'd have to send her a dream to be sure, but Venero was convinced that he found Gemma appealing because she was mortal.

If a dragon shifter.

Her gaze locked with his. "A Sword Sister finishes any matter her companion has left undone."

Venero couldn't stop himself from retreating at that, but he tried to disguise his trepidation by hopping toward the pool of water. "I see. How interesting."

"Do you know why Urbanus had her killed?"

"You know about that?"

Gemma smiled with complete confidence in her source of information. "Why do you think I accepted his suit?"

Venero was glad to have the truth out in the open. She'd married Urbanus to avenge Arista, which put them in alliance against his twin. "You could have had another reason."

Gemma averted her gaze, hiding some detail from him. Venero considered his words with care, wishing even as he did so that he and Gemma could be completely honest with each other. She was as slow to trust as he was. It was a trait that he might have found amusing to have in common with her, if he hadn't been thinking about how much easier it would be for her to kill him in his current form.

He cleared his throat. "You might have loved him."

Gemma laughed. "A prince of Regalia and a sorcerer? I might as well marry a MindBender or a DreamCaster!"

That told Venero all he needed to know about her view of him. It might be a good moment to remind her of his usefulness. "Arista stole something from the Grotto in the Citadel."

She bent down to hold his gaze, her own eyes glittering with determination. "And then?"

"She escaped."

Gemma arched a brow. "But you didn't."

"Someone had to defend her back." Venero's voice dropped low as he remembered being caught, being tormented, and being cursed. It had been the lowest point of his life, but at least Arista had escaped. That detail had given him strength. He knew the loss of the ShadowCaster had been a blow to his mother's ambitions.

Gemma shook her head. "I have a hard time believing that a toad was of much help to Arista."

"A toad has helped you," Venero replied. "Did you have to welcome Urbanus on your wedding night?"

"No."

"Did you know about the spelldust, and the pegasus, and that the antidote could be found in the Queen's Grotto of the Citadel? Did you know about the tunnel through the mountains?"

Gemma fell to her knees before him, and Venero had a hard time remembering what he'd meant to say. Her eyes shone, so clear a blue that he thought a man could drown in their depths. "You're right," she breathed and his anger faded...like magic. "I did need your help and I still do." She smiled and he couldn't take a full breath. "Thank you for helping Arista. Even though she was hunted in the end, I'm glad she got away. She might have fulfilled her other quest after all."

"Her quest? Wasn't she supposed to kill one of the princes?" Venero pretended not to have the details, although he knew very well what Arista had been hired to do.

Gemma nodded. "Venero. The twin brother of Urbanus. The DreamCaster who disappeared. I wonder if she succeeded." She winced. "She said she loved him and didn't know what to do."

"Caught between duty and love?"

"Apparently so. I was surprised."

Maybe she'd known that Arista was an android. "Maybe she let him escape."

Gemma fixed him with a look. "I thought you were with her. Wouldn't you have seen if she had?"

Venero averted his gaze. "I tend to fall behind when people move quickly. I miss some bits."

"That's understandable. I'm sorry I abandoned you on the path." Gemma smiled with a warmth that made his heart flutter. "I'm sorry I insulted you, too."

"Well, I was wrong, and I've provoked you, too." Venero stole a glance at her nude perfection, felt his blood heat, and knew he was wrong about a lot of things. "Demure" had a decided lack of appeal in Gemma's presence.

He was starting to like "forthright," "smart," and "determined."

He wondered if he could even come to like "dragon." There was something about this dragon princess of Incendium that challenged all of his assumptions.

And Venero liked it.

Gemma's eyes twinkled. "I was wrong, too." She dropped her voice to a whisper. "I missed you," she confessed, her voice husky.

Venero opened his mouth to say something and, for the first time since he had become a toad, croaked instead.

Gemma laughed lightly. She inhaled then and scanned the chamber, then turned to him again. He could see the dragon, and it troubled him, given that she was pledged to finish whatever her Sword Sister had left undone. Her eyes were glittering again and her gaze was locked on him.

"Something the matter?"

"The Seed," Gemma whispered, almost to herself. "I smell the Seed again. How can that be?" What was she talking about? She bent toward him with purpose. "You were at the hut, in the satchel. You were in the bridal chamber. It's *you*."

"Me?"

"The Carrier of the Seed," she breathed.

Venero stared into her eyes and yearned for something he couldn't have, that he might never have again. His throat worked. He knew this was a moment to ask for one thing from her, but he couldn't do it. He couldn't make a sound.

When Gemma leaned down and kissed him, he couldn't believe his luck.

His reaction to the touch of Gemma's soft lips on his skin was pleasure, and desire... and then Venero felt a ripple pass through his body that grew to a quake. It was followed by the first twinge of a pain he'd never thought to feel again.

Gemma had done it! She'd overcome her revulsion and kissed him.

She'd broken the spell.

Which meant that Gemma was his one true love.

She was also, incidentally, obligated to complete Arista's mission to kill him.

Venero's thoughts spun even as the pain shot through his body. There was no time to think about the ramifications of what she'd accomplished. He didn't want her to witness the agony of his transformation. That sight might change everything between them forever. So, he croaked again, and then he hopped, jumping right into the basin of water and swimming hard until he was out of her view. The pavofel leaped to the lip of the pool and swiped into the water with one paw, but missed.

Venero swam with all his might. He made it through the opening that fed the water into the chamber before the shift began.

He could only hope that this time, the agony would be easier to endure.

He knew better than to expect it to be of shorter duration.

Urbanus would have been thorough like that.

It had been such a perfect conclusion. Gemma had been sure she was right. The toad had admitted to being enchanted. The scent of the Seed was strongest in his presence. He had to be the Carrier of the Seed, the prince whose truth was hidden, her destiny and her HeartKeeper.

But nothing happened when she kissed him.

Except that he fled.

Gemma was disappointed. She'd kissed him between those amber eyes, right on the white dot on his brow, and his skin had been dry and cool to the touch. It hadn't been that awful to kiss him, after all.

He'd looked at her, without blinking, for a moment as if she'd surprised him.

Then he'd croaked and jumped into the pool of water. He'd disappeared so quickly that she had the sense he was running away from her.

Or from her kiss.

Gemma supposed he wouldn't be the first creature to discover that he disliked what he said he wanted, but she was disappointed in him all the same.

At least he'd given Felice something to do. The pavofel was crouched on the lip of the pool, tail thrashing as she watched for any sign of the toad.

If he wasn't the Carrier cursed to take another form, then why could she smell the Seed again? Wasn't she alone?

Gemma checked the chamber and the tunnels for other intruders, but didn't find anyone despite an extensive search. She shivered, realizing the cavern had become chilly. She wrapped herself in her cloak and ate lightly from the provisions as she planned a strategy without the toad. Somehow she'd have to find her way through the mountain to the Citadel, then find the Queen's Grotto, then identify the antidote. No doubt there would be someone defending the route or the destination, or both. A little insider information would have been welcome, but the toad was gone. Maybe she'd see him again. Maybe not.

Had Urbanus pursued them? She had to think he would.

She had to be prepared.

Gemma rose and began to paint the marks on her own flesh in preparation for battle. If Arista's ghost had been with her, that spirit was gone. She felt very much alone, and keenly aware that there was no one to paint her back. She turned in place when the marks were as complete as she could make them and felt some frustration at her vulnerability.

How foolish to miss a toad. She was losing her good sense on this planet. The sooner she could get her dragon back and leave Regalia, the better.

She needed that antidote, and nothing was going to stand in her path.

Venero writhed on the floor of another cavern, his body wracked with pain. The transition seemed to take an eternity, two eternities, nine thousand times longer than it had taken the first time.

His limbs stretched until he wanted to scream. He swore he could feel every cell double, triple, grow to ten times its length. Then it would snap and divide, and repeat the process again. He had never been in such anguish in his life. His innards churned as they regained their former shape and dimensions, and Venero bared his teeth in agony. He dared not make a sound, lest he alert Gemma to his condition.

He didn't want anyone to see him like this.

No. He really didn't want *Gemma* to see him like this. He didn't want her to decide that he was weak or unworthy or—worst of all—revolting. And so, he curled on the floor of the cave and endured a pain that he began to fear would never end.

His skin smoothed and stretched, changing color and texture. Hair sprouted, so slowly that it was excruciating, on his head, his chest, his legs. The cut on his arm from the pavofel's bite became proportionately larger and the wound opened again, stinging as it bled blue once more. It was the least of his troubles. He bit back a moan as the torment increased to a crescendo and he was sure he couldn't stand any more. He opened his mouth to bellow and suddenly, his body quivered and stilled.

Venero took a deep breath.

He opened his eyes, then smiled at the sight of his hands and forearms. He sat up, running his hands down his legs and over his own torso, needing to feel the evidence that his human form was restored as well as to see it. He shoved a hand through his hair, savoring its thick waves as he never had before. He was covered with perspiration and well aware of the dirt beneath his nails. He was naked, too. He moved away from Gemma's refuge and immersed himself in the river that ran through the mountain. He scrubbed himself clean in its cold water and barely kept from laughing aloud.

Gemma had done this for him.

Gemma deserved a reward.

Wait. First, he had to send her a dream.

First, he had to verify that she didn't share Arista's nature.

He would have planned it better if he hadn't had such a grueling day. Or maybe it was magic, showing a quirk of its own. Maybe it was the last of his brother's influence.

But the fact remained that Venero sent Gemma a dream of the memory he was most trying to avoid.

And worse, because he wasn't as focused on his task as would have been ideal, Gemma experienced the moment as Arista would have remembered it. As soon as the dream left Venero, he regretted it. It was sloppy DreamCasting, no matter how he looked at it.

Turned out he was a bit out of practice.

But maybe there was another reason that Venero sent Gemma a dream of Arista's invitation to him. Maybe he thought it a mistake, but maybe, his magic knew better.

As reluctant as he was to share his secrets, Venero's magic might have known that Gemma would never fulfill her destiny as his true love without knowing a little bit more.

The flames of the candles flickered in a slight breeze within the cave, their light seeming to bring the fresh symbols on the wall to life. She had brought the dye to perform the ritual, but had never anticipated finding a cave so perfect. Her heart glowed that her companion had ensured it was so.

The marks appeared to undulate on the walls once the circle was complete, or even to dance. As she watched, as fascinated as ever, one morphed into another, their meaning changing before her very eyes. She could feel her companion's sense of wonder and was encouraged that they had this response in common. No matter how many times she painted the marks, they still filled her with awe.

With a fingertip, she made the last mark on the wall, the mark of her name. It glowed for a moment, as if the dye was filled with sparks, and a flame seemed to pass around the perimeter of the cavern.

"It is done," she whispered, hearing her companion turn in place to look.

She began to paint the symbols on her own skin, humming as she entered the meditative state suitable for this ritual. The dye flowed from her fingertip, forming the traditional shapes as if they were destined to be. The cave was charged with a sense of promise and possibility. She was aware of her companion watching her, and the hair seemed to tingle on the back of her neck.

It wasn't the only part of her that tingled.

When she was done, she lifted her hands high over her head and looked up at them. Her fingers stretched toward the heavens, and her feet were dusty with the soil of Regalia.

"The marks echo the transition from sky to earth, representing all the elements I will bring to bear when I enter battle," she informed her companion, who walked around her, looking. She preened. "Together, they form a coat of armor, a skin of ink and symbol, that will focus my spirit and protect me at war."

She turned in place, displaying herself proudly. There were intricate pentacles painted on the palms of her hands, then stars and moons flowed down her arms. Wings were painted on her shoulders and coiling snakes wound around her torso to her belly, where the open mouth of a great serpent surrounded her navel. Flowers and leaves were painted on her hips and thighs, with the waves of the sea frothing about her calves. A starfish was painted on the top of each foot, and a turtle on the bottom of each one.

"These are the ancient marks of the Warrior Maidens of Cumae," she whispered, then offered the small cup of dye. "They are modified for each of us, to better defend us in our specific vulnerabilities."

"I didn't think you had any vulnerabilities."

"Is that why you are so wary of me?"

"It's disconcerting, to say the least."

"You're in no hurry to share your vulnerabilities."

He laughed. "Stupidity isn't one of them."

"Do you distrust everyone?"

"Just those I can't anticipate."

"What if I choose to trust you? Would that reveal more of what you could anticipate from me?" She smiled when he didn't reply, and turned her back on him. "Will you continue the patterns, that my back is defended as well?"

She felt that warm fingertip, tracing the talons of great birds upon her shoulder blades, beneath the lines that echoed feathered wings. The talons would be grasping the uppermost coil of the great serpent and she closed her eyes, welcoming the power of all these predators within her.

By the time her back was covered in symbols, her breath was coming quickly and she was aroused, but not just from the ritual and the promise of battle. Her companion's fingertip lifted from her skin just as she felt the shimmer of heat that marked the completion of the body's preparation.

"They're on fire!"

"Not yet." She took a deep breath, and she turned around for the last mark.

The one that would be painted on her brow. The one that should have opened her third eye to the possibilities of the future. The one that should allow her to anticipate and see beyond the moment. The one that should set her aflame, all the same.

Even at the sight of him, an unruly desire heated her blood, and she awakened to a possibility she'd never considered before. She was maiden and warrior, her chastity part of her power, her duty all that defined her. But this man made her think for the first time of what she sacrificed in the pledge she'd made.

Until this assignment, companionship had been sufficient.

In this moment, Arista wanted more.

He was a fine man, but it was more than that. His chestnut hair hung to his shoulders, wavy and thick. His nose had been broken at some point in time and had healed with a slight kink. He was taller than she and his shoulders were broad, his body taut and strong. His gaze was steady, he spoke only truth, and he was both resolute and steadfast. He'd shown his valor and she trusted him, trusted him more than she had ever trusted anyone other than her Sword Sister. His eyes were the hue of amber and when their gazes locked, she knew her choice was made.

He was a warrior through and through, just like her. He was still dressed, though his weapons had been laid aside. He honored her ritual but did not intrude. He was her companion in this world, her guide, and her ally.

But he had also stolen her heart.

She would not enter this battle as a maiden.

Whatever the price, the sacrifice would be worth it.

She leaned closer, placed one hand on his shoulder, then reached to brush her lips across his. She felt his surprise. She thought it irrelevant. "I am yours for the taking, Venero," she whispered. "After this night, I will be a maiden no more."

Venero knew that there was no point regretting the dream.

What was done was done.

And the good news was that Gemma *did* dream.

She might feel the need to kill him, but she wasn't an android. And he might have a fighting chance in a battle between them, since her dragon was currently unavailable.

Venero shook the water out of his hair and strode toward the cavern where Gemma slept, filled with vigor and purpose. It was so good to be back in his familiar form, and to have the powers back that he had once taken for granted. He felt clean and whole and strong. He took great satisfaction in how quickly he covered the distance to the cavern where Gemma had taken refuge.

He wanted to see her again.

He wanted her to see him.

The pavofel met him on the threshold and looked him up and down. Its tail flicked and its whiskers twitched, but it didn't even try to block his path. Instead, it strolled to the other side of the cavern and curled up to sleep.

Venero grinned that he didn't look like such easy prey anymore. He turned to consider Gemma and his chest tightened.

Warrior and woman. How could he have imagined that he wanted anyone less.

Gemma was curled in a cloak in the middle of the cavern and he was glad that she had fallen asleep. A candle burned below the medallion painted on the walls, the one that had Arista's mark. That Gemma was asleep gave him a chance to look at her, to admire her, to observe her. She stretched and murmured, his name upon her lips.

Venero smiled. He could see the painted marks on Gemma's feet where they emerged from beneath the warmth of the cloak, and he eased closer. Had she painted herself as Arista had done?

He wanted to see.

No, he burned to see.

Venero lifted the cloak slowly, revealing Gemma's nudity to his gaze. He surveyed the marks that adorned her skin, smiling at their familiarity, noting their differences. He saw her take a sharp breath. She frowned and he feared the worst, then suddenly she rolled over. Venero's smile returned when he realized she'd turned her back to him.

It was a gesture that spoke of trust.

Of welcoming a companion she trusted to defend her back.

The little pot of dye was set to one side, and there was still dark liquid in it. Gemma's back was devoid of the symbols that covered the rest of her skin, but Venero knew what had to be done.

He wasn't her Sword Sister, not by any means, but he

would help. He'd done this before, after all.

And if Gemma made the same offer that Arista had, Venero wouldn't decline.

CHAPTER SIX

Gemma awakened with the conviction that she wasn't alone.

She kept her eyes closed and reviewed what had to have been a dream. She wasn't sharing the cavern with a man—much less one so handsome as the one she'd just seen—and she had lit only one lantern in the cavern. In her dream, she had sounded like Arista, and her figure had been boyish like that of Arista. Her thinking had shown the crisp precision that she associated with Arista.

She had dreamed of Arista's night in this cave.

With Venero.

Had Arista really offered herself to him? If Gemma hadn't shared the thoughts of her Sword Sister, she wouldn't have believed it possible. Arista had been less emotional than any of the other Warrior Maidens, and her dedication to her trade had been beyond question.

But this Venero had changed her mind.

By stealing her heart.

The power of Arista's love had been compelling. Gemma wished she had dreamed a little more. What was it like to fall in love? How had Venero's kiss felt? Was sex different when you were in love?

Gemma took a deep breath and smelled the skin of another person. The hair prickled on the back of her neck and she wished she could shift shape to surprise the intruder. Irritation rose within her at Urbanus for cheating her of her most powerful gift. Fortunately, she had other skills. She listened, feigning sleep, and waited.

Where was Felice?

Gemma heard the cup of dye scrape against the stone. The intruder was lifting it, perhaps sniffing it, trying to identify its contents.

She heard a soft step as he or she approached, then was surrounded by the scent of the Seed. Before she could clear her thoughts, a fingertip landed on her back.

It was warm. It was wet. It traced the curve of a feather, the kind of feathers that Arista had chosen to defend the backs of her shoulders. Gemma caught her breath.

The Carrier had come to her. Her heart swelled.

"Hold still, sleeping beauty," a man said, his voice low with humor. "I've only done this once before."

His finger moved with confidence, belying his words, and Gemma blinked.

He sounded like the man in her dream.

"Venero?"

"Guilty as charged," he admitted and the echo of the toad's words made Gemma smile.

She sat up and turned, only to find the man from her dream squatted behind her. He smiled crookedly, his eyes gleaming amber and warm with appreciation. He had broken his nose once. He was tall and powerful. He was no toad, even if his eyes were the same glorious hue.

He was nude and she stole a glance, appreciating how muscled and trim he was. A splendid male specimen, if a little pale. Her mouth went dry, then she noticed the cut on his forearm. It was healing, and the scab was a deep blue crust.

It was in the same place as the wound Felice had given the toad.

He returned her gaze steadily, unflinchingly. "Thanks, Gemma," he murmured.

The missing prince of Regalia had been found.

He was her HeartKeeper.

And he didn't believe in love.

"You were here with Arista," Gemma charged, hating that she sounded so breathless.

That she felt so keenly aware of him. It made her sound foolish, more like a demure maiden than the warrior she knew herself to be. She tugged the cloak around herself, as if the fabric could defend her from his allure.

"I was." Venero sobered and looked down at the color dripping from his fingertip. "How remarkable to have a second Warrior Maiden of Cumae arrive in this cave."

"I'm not technically one of them anymore."

"Are you here to avenge her?" He arched a brow. "Or finish what she started?"

"That depends." Gemma admitted. "Were you lovers?"

Venero's grin was quick and reassuring. "I have no interest in androids." He shuddered a little. "I like my women warm and mortal, as well as beautiful."

Gemma didn't smile. "What are you talking about?"

"Arista was an android," he said with conviction. "An excellent android of superior design and manufacture, but a machine all the same."

"No!"

"Yes."

"She wasn't an android," Gemma insisted. "I knew her for years. We were Sword Sisters! We trusted each other completely."

Venero held her gaze, his confidence complete. "Just because you didn't know doesn't mean it wasn't true."

"Just because you have a suspicion doesn't mean you're right. You can't be sure."

He nodded once. "I am."

"How can you be?"

He pursed his lips and looked down at the cup. "Her mind was different. You must have sensed that."

"She was a precise thinker. Always logical."

Venero looked up. "She didn't dream, Gemma."

Gemma frowned, thinking of her own dream, but Venero continued before she could speak.

He stepped closer and the scent of the Seed nearly overwhelmed her. "I liked her," he admitted in a whisper. "I admired her." His gaze swept over Gemma as surely as a touch. "But I need to be able to trust a lover."

Her heart skipped at the implication of that, but she kept talking about Arista. This was her chance to learn more. "You couldn't trust a woman you believed to be an android?"

"I didn't believe it: I knew it," he corrected. "And that meant I didn't know what price she might be willing to pay for success. I knew she was programmed to fulfill her mission."

"Did you know what it was?"

"To kill me, of course. I knew about that before she arrived."

"How?"

His smile was wry. "My mother is easy to anticipate but harder to stop." He shook his head. "But there was something else Arista came to do, and I sensed that it was more important than the assignment to kill me."

"So you helped her."

"And I paid the price." He smiled and it was easy to see how he'd captured Arista's heart. If she'd met him in this form, Gemma wouldn't have delayed that kiss, especially not with the scent of the Seed arousing her as it did. He put down the cup of dye and took a step closer.

Gemma waited, wanting whatever he was going to offer. "I was trapped, until you came along and saved me."

"Meaning true love does exist after all?"

He frowned, looking so concerned that Gemma wanted to make him smile again.

"Are you sure it will stick?" she asked, her tone teasing. "Maybe I should kiss you again to be sure."

"Maybe," he replied with a laugh. His eyes shone as he regarded her, and he beckoned with a fingertip. His voice dropped low. "Come here, Gemma." She moved willingly into his arms, her heart skipping in anticipation. His gaze fell to her lips and she smiled, lifting her hands to his shoulders. He bent toward her and Gemma reached up for his kiss.

"Thank you, Gemma," Venero whispered, just before his lips brushed across hers. A tingle swept through Gemma and her desire surged. She reached for him, catching the back of his neck in her hand, and kissed him. It was a long and passionate kiss, one worthy of a reward, and when Venero lifted his head, Gemma's heart was racing.

She stared into his golden eyes and was assailed by a curious sensation. Her pulse matched to his, the feel of their hearts pounding in unison enough to make her dizzy. The scent of the Seed filled her with urgency. She saw Venero's eyes brighten and couldn't look away. He swallowed visibly, then pulled her close, crushing her against his chest. The sensation grew more powerful.

He lifted his hand to her chin. "What's happening?" he murmured and she knew he could feel it, too. "Is this love?"

Gemma smiled and shook her head. "It's my dragon. You're the Carrier of the Seed," she whispered. "We're destined lovers."

"And that means there will be a son?" His arms tightened around her and she wanted to explore his body fully. His skin was warm and his body firm. Gemma reached down and caressed him. He caught his breath and smiled, his hand sliding down to tease her breast.

"A son," Gemma agreed, remembering his earlier words but needing to say it anyway. "It also means that you're my HeartKeeper."

Venero was bending to take her nipple in his mouth but looked up. "I told you that I don't believe in love."

How could he, given that he had a mother who ordered his assassination and a twin brother like Urbanus? "You should reconsider. It's how I saved you, after all."

"There is that." He gave her that lazy smile and her heart skipped. "Maybe I'll have to restore your dragon first."

"I thought you liked your women demure."

Venero laughed. "You're changing my mind, Gemma." They stared into each other's eyes as the Seed urged Gemma's desire to a fever pitch. She had a feeling that even without the Seed's scent, she'd want Venero with his smile and his irreverent comments, his challenges and his valor. She liked that he was concerned about doing the right thing, even at his own expense. She admired that he teased and provoked her, tempting her smile and her laughter. It would never be boring to live with Venero.

"You're changing my mind about everything," he whispered. His thumb moved across her skin, setting her afire, and she wanted all of him, immediately. "What happens next?"

"That's easy," she replied. "This." Gemma framed Venero's face in her hands and stretched to kiss him. Heat fired through her from the point of contact with his mouth, and she tasted his gasp of surprise that she was so demanding. Then his hands were in her hair and he was pulling her closer. His kiss deepened and she could taste his need. Gemma welcomed it, responding to the passion he kindled without question.

And wanting only more.

Venero couldn't understand why he'd ever thought it was a bad thing for a woman to be forthright or outspoken or demanding. Gemma's kiss was fierce and decisive, and her unmistakable desire for him was the strongest aphrodisiac in the galaxy. He knew exactly where he stood with her, and it was a fine place to be.

Venero found himself deepening his kiss and meeting her demands for more. His blood was aflame and any plans he'd had to seduce her slowly—to savor her—went up in smoke.

That she was nude and at ease with that only fanned the flames. That she knew what she wanted from him and wasn't shy about making her wishes clear was enough to incinerate his reservations—and his assumptions. Her kiss was hot and hungry, and he was as consumed with her as she seemed to be with him. He could sense the dragon in her kiss and her passion was incredibly exciting.

He backed her against the wall of the cavern and kissed her deeply, loving how she knotted her hands in his hair and pulled him closer. She rubbed herself against him, then reached down to caress him, her touch both confident and gentle. He heard himself moan, then felt Gemma's chuckle.

"I knew you were naked for a reason," she whispered then dropped to her knees. Venero found his fingers in the silk of her hair as she tormented him with the softness of her lips and the occasional brush of her teeth. He whispered her name, knowing he wouldn't last long before such an assault, and felt her laugh again. She flicked her tongue across the tip of his erection, sending a shiver of delight through his entire body.

He looked down to find her eyes dancing, even as she gripped his hips. She held his gaze, inviting him to watch her caress him, and Venero knew he'd never seen a sight so arousing in his life. His entire body was humming. His blood was pumping. His erection was so large and hard that it ached. He felt like a bow drawn taut, and that the merest flick would send him over the edge. He couldn't tear his gaze away from Gemma's. Their hearts did that dizzying feat of matching pace again, and he felt lost in the marvel that was Gemma.

And he didn't care.

"I was going to thank you," he managed to whisper.

Gemma teased him with the tip of her tongue. "Now or later?"

"Now," he said, because he knew he'd only last another second if she stopped. "In a most fundamental way."

"How?"

"With pleasure."

Gemma smiled. "I like that kind of thanks."

Venero bent and caught her upper arms in his grip, then kissed her again. He spun her around the room, as if they were dancing at court, and she laughed into his kiss. Her hair floated behind them, long and golden, and she was a graceful dancer.

He kicked her feet out from beneath her, then caught her in his arms, liking how her eyes glowed as he lowered her to the pile of her discarded clothing. She was so beautiful that he wanted to play homage to her forever. Gemma gasped when he took the tight peak of her nipple in his mouth, and moaned softly when he teased her with his tongue and teeth. She arched her back, her nipple getting harder and the scent of her arousing him even more. Venero wanted to watch her, as well as pleasure her. She wasn't shy and she welcomed his touch with a confidence he found enticing.

She was bold and demanding and passionate—just as a dragon should be.

He rolled her to her back then, spreading her thighs so he could give her a more intimate kiss. Gemma sighed and welcomed him, purring in pleasure when his tongue landed upon her. Their hearts beat as one as he teased her, alternating little nips with languid strokes as her passion rose. He loved how he could feel her reaction as keenly as his own, how he could time his actions to increase her arousal, how well he could torment her with pleasure. He drove her high and halted just before she had her release, then did it again. Gemma was writhing beneath him, moaning and whispering his name. He could feel that her skin was hot and her heart was racing. She was slick and ready when Venero bent to make her reward complete.

"No," she said, her hand blocking him. He looked up to find her eyes shining. "With you," she insisted.

Venero didn't need to be invited twice. He moved over the length of her, running a trail of kisses to her shoulder. She wrapped her legs around his waist and he eased into the tight heat of her. She groaned with pleasure as he buried himself completely and he had to pause to catch his breath. Then her nails were digging into his shoulders in silent demand and her need drove him on. They moved together, gazes locked and breath matched, the heat rising between them so rapidly that Venero lost track of everything.

Save the woman in his arms.

And when they reached the summit together, crying out in unison as the fire of release raced through their bodies, Venero knew there was no going back after a mating with a dragon princess. She was unlike any other woman he'd ever known. The experience had been a hundred times more potent than ever before. He felt as if he'd been waiting for her, and that now, no other woman would do.

True love.

Who would have guessed it possible? Not Venero.

He smiled as he dozed, realizing that even though Gemma didn't believe in magic, she was very adept at casting a spell.

Gemma remained awake while Venero slept. Now that the influence of the dragon was diminished and the call of the Seed had been answered, doubts assailed her.

She should, as Arista's Sword Sister, fulfill Arista's unfinished assignment of assassinating Venero.

She should also make a permanent bond with Venero because he was her HeartKeeper. She could sacrifice Arista's mission for her HeartKeeper, but Gemma wondered. Would Venero ever believe in love? Could she teach him?

Could she trust a man who was a DreamCaster?

Or should she just be content with having the Seed? She wasn't good with compromise, so that wasn't an appealing option.

If they reached the Queen's Grotto and broke the spell over Gemma's dragon, what was Venero's plan? What were his intentions?

Gemma didn't know.

And that meant she couldn't lie quietly beside him any longer.

She rose to her feet and began to pack for the day ahead. Gemma watched Venero as he slept and felt uncharacteristic doubt about her future.

He would be the father of her son, and according to the prophecy, King of Regalia. Did that mean that she had a future with him or not? Should she tell him about the prophecy or not?

If she asked him for the whole truth, would he tell her?

There was only one way to find out.

Venero awakened with an overwhelming sense of well-being. He stretched and reached for Gemma, only to discover that she had left his side.

That was disappointing. He liked morning sex.

He opened his eyes to see her crouched before him, packing the satchel. He wondered whether she meant to leave him, but she wasn't dressed.

She spoke to him without turning around, so he knew she must have detected the change in his breathing. "Will you paint my back, please?" Gemma pivoted on the balls of her feet, presenting the cup of dye. Her expression was cool and inscrutable.

What had she decided?

"So long as you don't want to be defended from me." The question was meant to be teasing, but he felt her attention sharpen.

Her blue eyes were glittering, looking once again as if they were made of faceted sapphires, and he was reminded a little too well of her lost abilities. There was still a dragon within her, even if her power to shift had been suppressed.

"Should I be?" she asked, her voice low enough to make him shiver.

Venero felt exposed as he seldom had before, at least outside of his brother Celo's presence. He averted his gaze and rose, then made every sign of stirring the dye with his fingertip. It didn't need his undivided attention, but he feared that if he met Gemma's gaze, she'd see clear through to his soul.

There were some secrets he still needed to keep.

"Of course not."

Gemma turned her back upon him, but there was a tension in her. He could almost hear her thoughts spinning. He wished he knew what she was thinking. She was wary, but she needed him for this task. Maybe that was the best he could hope for.

He was more disappointed by that than he felt he should have been.

Venero worked in silence, wondering all the while how he could win Gemma's trust. He drew protective wings on her shoulders, then considered what else she had done. Instead of the snake coiled around her waist, she had rows of scales. And she'd drawn a tail, that wrapped around her left leg to her ankle.

Of course, her marks would include her true nature.

He drew a spiked ridge down her spine, then extended those wings into claws, like those of a bat. He'd never seen her in her dragon form, so he guessed. He noticed the water swirling around her lower legs, and the clouds on her upper arms. When she turned to face him, he saw that there was a cluster of gems around her navel. He impulsively drew a crown upon her forehead.

With a jewel in the middle of her brow.

She watched him closely as he painted, but he kept his attention fixed on his fingertip. He finished the crown, then paused before finishing the oval of the gem.

He couldn't avoid her steady gaze then.

"Can you read my thoughts?" she asked.

"Why would you think that?"

"It's prudent to know the abilities of your comrades before entering a battle."

Venero had to acknowledge that she was right, even though he wished she wanted to know for a more romantic reason. That should have been more troubling than it was. He'd never yearned for an emotional bond before. All his life, he'd been content to follow his own course and be self-reliant. He'd been satisfied with the conquest of a woman who intrigued him every time. Sex once, or maybe twice, had always satisfied him.

But he looked at Gemma, her hair loose and her skin

adorned with protective symbols, her gaze clear as she studied him, and he wanted her even more than he had the day before.

HeartKeeper. It was a surprisingly appealing notion.

"No, I can't," he admitted. "Only Celo can do that."

Gemma met his gaze, inviting more.

"My youngest brother. The one who helped you in the forest."

"I heard that you each have some magical ability and yours is DreamCasting."

"You already know that."

"But not exactly what that means." She smiled a little. "Remember that I don't understand magic well."

Venero nodded, unable to dismiss the sense that his answers were critical. She was watching him a little too closely. "I can send dreams to others while they sleep. Sometimes, I can send thoughts to others while they're awake."

"Like MindBending."

"It's similar. Less persuasive. More restricted." He sighed and tried to explain. "No one's born with the ability to DreamCast. It's a gift and it's defined at the point of giving."

"By the giver?"

He nodded. "MindBending is an inborn talent. It can be developed and refined, expanded even." He shrugged. "It's a lot more powerful."

"So, you can't read the thoughts of others?"

Venero frowned. "Only my twin brother, once in a while when he's careless—or excited about something. It's only happened a couple of times."

"But might be useful."

"It might be."

"And you can still influence the choices of others."

Venero saw that she didn't like that idea at all, but he wouldn't lie. "That's right."

Gemma's next words were low. "Have you ever done that to me?"

Venero opened his mouth then closed it again. She was watching him closely, so closely that he wondered how many of his secrets she could perceive. Maybe honesty between them should start immediately. Maybe it was time to take a chance. "Yes." He saw her gaze flicker. "I sent you the dream of Arista's memory. Nothing else."

"So that I'd trust you when you appeared." She surveyed the cavern, a little too composed for his taste. Venero never thought he'd want a woman to show more emotion, but Gemma was impassive. On the other hand, he respected that she was gathering all of the information before she responded.

As if she built a law case. That notion reassured him mightily.

"You sent me a dream of Arista's even though you saw she was an android."

"No, you dreamed a memory. I sent you a dream, but it wasn't a dream itself."

She smiled. "You sound like a lawyer."

"I am. I studied on Advocia. Good preparation for administration and negotiation."

"For a king."

Venero laughed. "For a diplomat, more likely." He knew better than anyone that Urbanus would be king after their mother's death, if that ever happened.

"But Arista loved you. I thought androids didn't feel emotions."

"They don't. She said she loved me, but that was just a strategic move. People confess love to get what they want..."

"Is that why you don't believe in love?"

"Well, I haven't experienced much love in my family."

"No wonder you doubt its existence. But I have,"

Gemma said, her eyes glowing. "And I know that with trust and love, everything is a thousand times better."

Her conviction was compelling but Venero wanted proof. "But how do you know? How can you be sure that the other person means what they say and that they don't just want something?"

Gemma pursed her lips, considering. "Because you trust them. Sometimes because they put the needs of the beloved above their own. You helped Arista escape, for example. Are you sure you didn't love her?"

"No, I didn't." Venero fell silent but Gemma was watching and waiting. "It was just the right thing to do. My mother needs to be challenged."

"Even if you have to pay the price."

"The greater good has to be served by someone." He forced a smile but Gemma didn't smile back at him.

"Why did you send me that dream? Was it strategic, to keep me from fulfilling Arista's mission as her Sword Sister?"

"No!" Venero was insulted by the implication and he saw immediately that Gemma had expected as much. "I made a mistake," he admitted with some irritability. "I'm out of practice. Plus there's something about writhing in pain that messes up my timing and control."

Gemma frowned. "Pain?" Her gaze swept over him, then lingered on the cut on his forearm. "I haven't hurt you that badly."

"It was the change. You, of all people, have to understand that."

She frowned at him, her confusion clear.

"When you kissed me and I shifted shape," Venero explained impatiently. "I don't know why you'd want to live with such an ability or why you would even do it. The shift is horrible. I've never felt such agony in my life, and..."

Gemma smiled. "Amateur," she said and Venero was

astonished to realize that she was teasing him.

More importantly, she wasn't angry with him.

"Amateur?" He pretended to be insulted, but he was intrigued by the sparkle in her eyes. He liked that she was giving as good as she got.

"It takes practice to shift with grace. *Endless* practice."

"I'd rather not."

"Coward." Her smile softened her charge.

He grinned back at her. "Absolutely." He made a grimace. "No more practice for me. I like being the way I am now just fine."

"And I thought princes of Regalia were intrepid," she scoffed.

"Even we have our limits." Their gazes held once again, and he felt that weird sense of their hearts matching pace. His own heartbeat felt amplified and it made him dizzy. "That's your dragon," he whispered and Gemma nodded. "I like that it does this."

"Me, too."

She was so at ease with her other form and its powers. And to tell the truth, Venero didn't have any issues with the abilities he might have credited to it so far. He found it sexy when Gemma was focused, and he liked how she fought. He liked watching her reason through a problem and her perceptiveness was impressive. He liked when her eyes glittered and this matching-heartbeats thing was incredible.

Having her on his side was a good thing.

Could she be right about love?

Gemma dropped her gaze to the cup of dye and offered it to him. "Will you finish the markings, please."

She was so serious that Venero wanted to make her smile. "Will the ritual work, even if completed by an amateur?"

"Only one way to find out." Gemma eyed him. "Afraid of failure?"

"No. Not me. I'm an intrepid prince."

"Even if I was a dragon again?" she asked softly.

"Even then," Venero said, and knew it was true as soon as he said it. Gemma watched him, inviting a reply. "Because I trust you," he admitted and her smile was all the reward he needed.

Venero closed the circle on her brow, then stepped back as the markings on Gemma's body appeared to erupt in flame. Fire blazed over her skin and she raised her hands over her head, just as Arista had done, reveling in the sensation. It seemed to him that the burn was hotter and brighter, maybe because of Gemma's true nature. The flame leaped from her fingertips, shooting a column of fire toward the roof of the cavern. Sparks showered over them, then the marks on the walls were illuminated. The fire spread around the cavern with dizzying speed, filling it with heat and light. Venero felt as if he were in the middle of an explosion, but it built to a crescendo then faded to a glow.

Like embers in the fire.

She was a splendid warrior and he wanted to see her in her dragon form. "What color are you, as a dragon?"

"You'll have to help me find the antidote to find out." Gemma's eyes shone and her smile was filled with confidence. "I want you again," she said, and Venero felt the acceleration of her pulse, as if her desire drove his own. It was so honest and so potent, this connection between them.

Hot, unquenchable, and a fire in his very soul.

If this was love, Venero only wanted more.

Their lovemaking wasn't as leisurely as the first time, though it was just as powerful.

They didn't linger but rose immediately to wash and dress. Gemma felt filled with purpose. She knew they were approaching danger and that they might not both survive whatever confronted them in the Queen's Grotto.

"Will Urbanus follow us?" she asked when she was dressing.

"I'm sure he already has." Celo had included a change of clothing in the satchel, and Venero donned that. There were shoes in addition to the boots that Gemma wore and he laced them with purpose.

"What are his powers?"

"They increase all the time. He's studying quite intensely under my mother and she keeps giving him more."

Gemma grimaced. "That's not very helpful."

Venero gave her a look. "We know he can cast spelldust, which immobilizes all it touches and makes those items or beings immune to the passage of time. We know he can concoct a spell to make you sleep. We know he blames me for Arista's escape."

"And we know he paid for her death. Was that because she escaped?"

"And because she stole something important."

"You didn't say what it was."

"She was after my mother's ShadowCaster."

"I thought ShadowCasters were extinct."

"Maybe there's one left."

"And she escaped with it." Gemma pursed her lips when he nodded. "I wonder what happened to it afterward."

"I'd have to think that it was retrieved when Arista was killed."

Now Gemma chuckled. "There's proof that you didn't understand Arista very well. No, once she claimed it, she would have ensured it couldn't be taken back."

Venero gave her a considering glance. "Could you guess where it is, then?"

"Probably not. She would have anticipated that my

understanding of her character and habits would be the weak link. She would have protected me with ignorance."

"It's not much protection if someone were to torture you for information you don't have."

Gemma considered the shadows in his eyes and wondered what had happened before he'd been turned into a toad. She wasn't sure she wanted to know, and she could see that he didn't want to talk about it. "You haven't trained on Cumae," she said gently. "The mission is always of highest importance. Ignorance means you can't weaken and fail. It's a great gift." She nodded toward the opening of the cave. "I smell the earth warming at the sun's first touch. We should continue."

Venero was glad of her keener senses. "Maybe you'll smell pursuit or guards before I do," he suggested, hefting the satchel. The pavofel watched them, then followed as he led Gemma onward. "The path goes up a little more and then descends. I don't expect to be noticed until we round the last couple of turns, but anything is possible."

"Can we talk?"

Venero considered that. "There could be spies."

Gemma nodded. "It's possible that your ability could be of use," she said. "Can you send me a better understanding of spells and antidotes? I may have to make quick decisions once we reach our destination, and it is always best to be prepared."

"Spoken like a Warrior Maiden striding into battle," he couldn't help but note.

"It's what I am," Gemma said and Venero realized the truth that her nature was what made him admire her so much.

Maybe he could have a future with a dragon princess.

He smiled at her and took her hand in his, then they walked onward together.

* * *

As they strode through the darkness beneath the mountain, Gemma held the lit candle ahead of them. The only sound was dripping water, their stealthy footfalls and the occasional stone loosed by their boots. Felice stayed closer than usual, her eyes gleaming in the darkness. The tunnel rose as Venero had said, then dipped again. Once it turned downward, it twisted more often, and they made slower time, because they checked around every corner before proceeding. Gemma was alert, her dragon senses strained for any sign of guards or spies.

All the while Venero's words spilled into her thoughts. He explained to her about the fabrication of spells, the necessary ingredients and the unnecessary additions that disguised the true intent of the spell caster. He discussed ingredients, showing an impressive knowledge of herbs and minerals. She knew he was only giving her an overview, with some examples to illustrate his points. He talked about the will of the victim, and turning it to the intent of the spell caster for, as he explained, it was easier to persuade anyone to do something he or she already desired to do—even if that desire was deeply secret.

He asked her to consider whether she had any buried urge to be rid of her dragon powers, and Gemma had to admit that as a young dragon still mastering her abilities, she had sometimes wished for a simpler life, one without such powers. She couldn't reply to Venero, and though he'd said he couldn't read her mind, she wasn't sure if that was true. She guarded her thoughts carefully, even before he discussed strategies for defending one's thoughts from sorcerers.

As they walked, she felt the Seed take root within her, her satisfaction growing with every step that she would bear Venero's son. It wasn't just the prospect of fulfilling her promise to her father that gave her such pleasure.

No, she liked Venero. She liked that he provoked and teased her. She liked that he was clever and intrepid. Even though she hadn't spent that much time with him, she respected that Arista had come to love him. He'd been wrong about Arista's nature, of course, but that had simplified matters between Gemma and Venero in the end. She would have found it troubling if he'd been her friend's lover.

Finally, he fell silent and Gemma realized how far they'd walked. They halted before a turn and she couldn't tell how much time had passed. Felice was tired, though, twining around her ankles as she did when she wanted to be carried. Gemma paused to pick up the pavofel and tucked her under one arm.

Venero was peeking around the corner ahead. He sighed and looked back at her, sending her one last bit of information.

The antidote will look like what it does. Venero shrugged when Gemma frowned. *I can't explain it better than that, but antidotes can't seem to fully hide what they are. There will be some kind of visual clue, probably linked to what Urbanus had in mind when he cast the spell. It might be his goal. It might be indicative of how he sees you. It might be what he fears about your ability. I just can't explain it better than that.* Venero paused. *You should know that sometimes, killing the spell caster breaks the spell yet at other times, it locks the spell in place for all eternity.*

"Nice," Gemma said aloud, clearly meaning the opposite.

We'll both look. Once we find it, grab it and run.

No. Gemma shook her head. Once she found the antidote, she was going to break the spell, breathe fire and fly. She gave Venero a crisp nod and they slipped around the corner, both watching for the inevitable confrontation.

Chapter Seven

I t was the strangest thing.

No one blocked their progress.

No one challenged them.

The Citadel appeared to be deserted.

That was more than enough to make Venero uneasy. Gemma moved forward with confidence, but Venero didn't believe it was possible to get this far into his mother's sanctuary without detection.

Especially as Urbanus had to be hunting them. Someone would have told him about the pegasus, even if he hadn't seen it in flight. Someone would have betrayed Venero and Gemma.

This was Regalia, after all.

But the gates of the Citadel stood open. The guard posts were abandoned. The late afternoon sky was clear blue and empty. It was as if a plague had swept through the land while they'd been under the mountain, and they were the last survivors.

Venero didn't believe that. His heart was racing as they strode onward, and a trickle of sweat ran down his back. It was a trick and he knew it, but he couldn't see what else to do other than make the most of an apparent opportunity. Gemma moved quickly, scanning their surroundings with impressive speed. They were through the empty courtyard, entering the massive open door, crossing the length of the glittering chamber when his mother received visitors.

The Citadel was as cold and silent as the grave.

He pointed to the hidden doorway and paused when he found it still locked.

He met Gemma's gaze. *It's probably enchanted, like the saddle.*

She nodded understanding and gestured impatiently to the lock. They would just have to make a run for it. Venero remembered the old code and hoped it worked. He whispered it and blew the words into the lock.

The tumblers turned.

The door seemed to ripple for a moment and he had time to fear the worst.

Then the door swung open without a sound, revealing a shadowed staircase.

Venero struck the flint and lit the last of their candles. The light didn't seem to spread as far as he thought it should, but that didn't surprise him. Not here.

Gemma was through the gap, watchful but fast. She claimed the candle and headed down the stairs with purpose. Venero hastened after her, scanning the stairs for watchful eyes. That he found none didn't reassure him at all. They reached the bottom and Gemma paused in astonishment.

The Queen's Grotto was a natural formation that had been augmented by Arcana over many years. It was an underground cave, made by water dripping on stone. Stalactites hung from the ceiling of the cavern, their crystalline points reflecting the gold of the candlelight and dripping toward the floor. Stalagmites rose from the floor of the cavern in jagged points, their roots surrounded in places by pools of black water. The formations had always looked like teeth to Venero, sharp teeth ready to shred the unwary visitor.

Like dragon teeth.

But they weren't all natural formations. They were repositories.

Venero didn't waste time in admiration. He started at the left and surveyed the first stalactite. When he found the symbol etched into it, he showed Gemma. She leaned closer and he wondered if she could see the antidote locked in the stone.

Then she stared in new wonder at the Grotto, her gaze darting from one symbol to another. *This many spells*, she mouthed, her outrage clear.

Venero sighed and nodded. *Welcome to Regalia.*

He was impressed that she didn't appear to be daunted. Her eyes shone with purpose. He began to work his way around the grotto from the left, examining each rock formation in turn. Gemma worked from the right. Even as they moved deeper into the Grotto, Venero was thinking that they'd both have to make a complete circuit. Whatever marked the antidote might not be obvious to either of them.

They might have to look at them together and join forces to solve the riddle.

Venero doubted they would have that much time.

At least, if he found the antidote first, he could send her the thought of it.

Venero wasn't going to think about what might be the consequence of that. Seeing Gemma fly free and knowing she'd conceived their son would be all the reward he needed.

He paused for a moment, considering this truth. He loved her. She really was his true love, and he, if they survived this ordeal, would willingly be her HeartKeeper. That realization gave Venero all the determination he needed to succeed.

It was obscene that a ruler could cast so many spells on her populace. Even if Arcana had used law and the courts to manage her people, this level of control was an abomination. No wonder the people were without will or purpose. They were defeated before they began. Perhaps that made them easier to govern, but it also enslaved them and cheated Regalia of the wealth and influence it might have, if its resources were encouraged to grow and prosper.

Even as she worked through the pillars of stone, Gemma felt her anger simmer. It was outrageous and it was wrong, and the planet needed to either crash into the sun or be ruled by someone utterly unlike Arcana.

Someone like Venero.

Someone who believed in progress and education, in justice and truth.

But Urbanus had cursed Venero once, and she doubted that either Urbanus or Arcana would be so lenient a second time.

Venero risked a lot in helping her.

He did it as it a matter of principle, she guessed. He would make a good king. They would make a good team ruling together, with her connections on Incendium and his vision for Regalia's future. She just had to ensure that he survived to fulfill his destiny.

"You were slower than I expected, Venero."

Gemma froze at the sound of a familiar and unwelcome voice.

"Perhaps your virtues are finally fading." Urbanus clucked his tongue. "Or maybe it's your vices growing."

"Good to see you, brother." Venero spoke calmly, sounding more at ease than he had to be.

Felice eyed him, her tail swishing, and Gemma bent to pick up her pet. Felice had been sitting against a stalagmite with a symbol burned into it in blood red.

It was the insignia of Incendium.

If that stone didn't contain the antidote for Gemma's state, it had to be a good one to break either way. She snapped it off in the act of picking up Felice and kept it in her hand, disguising it from view with the pavofel's long fur. Had there been a swirl of gold mist emanating from the broken stone?

She tried to shift shape, but had no more success than before.

At least she had a weapon now.

Urbanus descended the last steps and stood in the middle of the grotto. Gemma realized that it was like an arena, giving the person who stood at the middle a perfect view of the whole. Urbanus' voice also resonated and seemed to be amplified. "I really thought you'd keep your promise more quickly, brother."

Gemma frowned. Promise? Venero had promised Urbanus to bring her here? No! She didn't believe it. She looked at him, but he returned her stare steadily.

She understood that Urbanus would know if Venero sent her a thought.

But it did give her an excuse to deceive Urbanus.

"Oh, Urbanus!" Gemma cooed, hurrying toward him with Felice clutched tightly against her chest. "I'm so glad you're finally here. I was terrified when your brother took me captive!"

"He took you captive? When he was a toad?"

"Oh yes! He threatened to hit you again if I didn't go with him. I was so frightened when I saw you on the floor of your chamber....and the blood!" She gasped as if in recollection, well aware that Urbanus was studying her closely. "I'm terrified of toads! And he could speak! I didn't know what to do." She flung herself against his chest and looked up at him, lashes fluttering. "But now you're here and I'm safe."

Urbanus smiled and put his arm around her waist. "Yes, you are."

"Thank you, Urbanus, for saving me from the curse of my nature," Gemma said, letting her words fall in a rush.

He preened. "I knew you'd appreciate it, once you thought about it."

Mother has the antidote. Venero's words echoed clearly in Gemma's thoughts. *Marked with a flame.*

A thrill coursed through Gemma. But where was Queen Arcana?

"I heard that!" Urbanus shouted and snapped his fingers.

Gemma turned in time to see Venero was encased in a bubble. It encircled him, sealing him in place, and she guessed that he wouldn't be able to send her any more thoughts.

His expression was grim, and Gemma realized he'd anticipated this.

He'd taken the chance, for her.

The bubble looked to be made of similar stone to the formations that surrounded them, but as Urbanus continued to murmur, its diameter kept shrinking. Venero was forced to bend and then to crouch, and she saw him grimace as the stone tightened around him. It shimmered, then clouded, leaving only a clear crystal before Venero's face.

So he could watch. His lips set and his gaze was steady, as if he'd will Gemma to use the detail he'd sent her.

His own brother had done this to him. No wonder Venero didn't believe in love.

Urbanus beckoned and the stone ball containing Venero teetered between the stalagmites, then tumbled toward the middle of the cavern. It bounced then rolled to a stop before Urbanus. He halted its progress with one foot and his smile was filled with satisfaction. "Enough of your meddling, Venero. My wife and I will be happier without you around, making trouble." His smile was so smug that she wanted to cut it free.

Or fry it off.

She remembered Venero's warning about eliminating the spell caster. She was willing to risk it.

"Well done, husband." Gemma kissed Urbanus' throat and felt his resistance waver. "Let's go back to the palace," she purred. "Let's make our union complete." She felt Urbanus catch his breath. She rubbed herself against him and his hands landed on her shoulders. He bent toward her, his expression sultry and...

Felice chose that moment to protest being crushed between the pair of them. The pavofel hissed and Gemma stepped back, as if to console it. "Put down the creature, Gemma. Or better, leave it here. My mother has always wanted another pavofel. She'll take care of it."

"What a wonderful idea!" Gemma said, having no intention of doing that. She bent as if to put the pavofel on the ground and felt Urbanus come closer. She met Venero's gaze for a moment and let him see her resolve.

Venero blinked and Gemma knew Urbanus was right behind her. She spun and drove the broken piece of stone into his gut. The point slid into him far more easily than Gemma had expected, and she recalled how soft he was.

Urbanus fell back, staggering. "Gemma!" he cried, but she spun again, as Arista had taught her, and kicked him in the teeth.

Urbanus howled and fell backward, blue blood streaming from his mouth. "Witch!"

Gemma braced herself for attack when he growled and spun to his feet, fury in his eyes.

But then his expression changed and he scrambled to his feet, only to make a low bow.

Surely not to her.

The hair prickled on the back of Gemma's neck. She pivoted smoothly, and knew she shouldn't have been surprised to find Queen Arcana standing between the stalagmites. The monarch lifted her hands and clapped lightly, mocking Gemma with her applause. "I like a woman who is quick on her feet," she said, and Gemma doubted that was true. "Never mind one who keeps men in their place. Urbanus was always lazy about his physical training."

Gemma didn't ask about Venero.

"Help me, Mother," Urbanus said, holding his injured gut. The blood flowed from between his teeth, and also from his stomach. He stood in a puddle of blue blood, one that reminded Gemma of her first sight of the toad.

"That will depend upon your bride, and her cooperation."

"Gemma, I entreat you!" Urbanus said, then evidently realized the chance of Gemma helping him were slim indeed. He sank down to the floor, moaning quietly.

"Definitely not the stuff of kings," Arcana murmured, perhaps for Gemma's ears alone.

The queen smiled and strolled closer, holding her long dark skirts in her hands. "The time for games is passed, Gemma." She put out her hand imperiously. "Return it to me."

"Return what to you?"

"Your disobedience will only infuriate me." The queen smiled tightly. "Neither of us want to see that situation."

"But I don't know what you mean."

Queen Arcana sighed. "Very well. We shall play this your way." She strolled the length of the grotto, pausing to consider the pavofel. Felice stared back at her without blinking, as if the beast would provoke the queen deliberately. "I used to have a pavofel," she said. "I miss him so much. And this is a fine specimen."

"She is." Gemma picked up Felice again, not trusting the queen one bit.

"You could give her to me."

"I'm not feeling very generous right now." Gemma shrugged. "I might if I had a certain antidote." The truth was that she'd never abandon Felice, but the queen didn't need to know that.

"A wager then. How interesting." Queen Arcana made a circuit of the grotto, touching items idly, and Gemma guessed that the queen meant to distract her from something of import. She watched the queen with care, noting all the places the queen did not direct her gaze.

She had the antidote. But where was it hidden?

The queen gave the stone that contained Venero only the barest glance. "There should be enough air for him to see how this all ends," she murmured, and Gemma was horrified. "Of course, that depends upon you, Gemma."

Gemma straightened as Arcana turned to face her.

"You were the Sword Sister of Arista, a Warrior Maiden of Cumae, with whom you trained for several years," the queen said with authority. "She was here under false pretenses. She accepted a commission from me and failed to perform it because her true intent was the theft of a possession of mine. She only escaped because she was aided by my own son." Queen Arcana smiled. "Now you want something from me. You want your shifter powers back. I want the ShadowCaster back." She put out her hand again. "I think it would be a fair exchange."

"A ShadowCaster?" Gemma echoed, pretending this was the first she'd heard of Arista's theft. "They exist only in legend!"

"No. There is one that exists in truth. It was mine. It *is* mine, but the intruder stole it. I demand its return."

"Was Arista given that opportunity before she was killed?"

Queen Arcana smiled. "Of course. She insisted that

she had given it away, for safekeeping." Her voice dropped low. "Who better than a Sword Sister? You must have it. Give it to me."

Gemma knew that the ShadowCaster *was* safe, somewhere.

But she didn't have to admit that just yet.

"I don't have it." Gemma reached into her satchel and removed the *memoria*. "I found only this," she said then lied. "But it has no more power. I have to get it charged on Cumae to learn what Arista did with the ShadowCaster."

Queen Arcana snatched the *memoria* and studied it, trying to divine how to use it. She shook it to no avail. She tried to crack it open like an egg, but even the thin seam remained invisible. She whispered a spell to it, but nothing happened. She flung it back at Gemma so hard that Gemma wouldn't have caught it except for her dragon reflexes. "Open it!"

Gemma decided there was very little to be lost by following the command. She whispered Arista's code word to the *memoria*. Just as before, it took a long time to respond, and she feared it really had no power left.

Then it split and opened, moving more slowly than it had the first time. It spun in her palm and projected a hologram of Arista.

The image pulled to one side, distorted, and flickered.

"I don't know why I'm recording this," Arista confessed, just as before. But this time, the recording of her voice caught, crackled, and faded. The image dimmed even as Queen Arcana stepped closer, intent upon hearing every syllable. "Only my Sword Sister could ever view it..."

The hologram winked out, and the *memoria* closed.

"There must be more!" the queen insisted.

"Undoubtedly, but the device has no power. It must have had a faulty power supply in the first place. It can only be restored on Cumae."

The queen glared at her. "And only you can make the request."

Gemma shrugged.

"No, it's a trick," Urbanus said. "Don't let her go, Mother! She won't return and you'll lose the only chance we have of retrieving the ShadowCaster."

"We?" echoed the queen, turning upon her oldest son. "I wouldn't need to retrieve my ShadowCaster if you hadn't been such a fool." Her dark eyes narrowed. "I have to reconsider my assumption that you would become king, Urbanus."

"But..."

"You are proving to be a failure of the most colossal kind. Perhaps it is your father's legacy. He had little talent for leadership." She grimaced, waving off his protests. "First, you failed to guard your dreams, a particularly grievous error when I had entrusted you with the secret of the ShadowCaster."

"Of course, I *thought* about it. It was key to the future..."

"No doubt with the encouragement of Venero." Queen Arcana rose and approached her other son. "Who undoubtedly shared your dream with others, ensuring that the secret of the ShadowCaster was no longer a secret."

"Then Venero is the guilty party," Urbanus protested. "He must have wanted to compromise your power."

Queen Arcana turned to face him. "But he would not have had any revelations to share if you had guarded your dreams as you had been taught. You were the origin of the problem." She held up a second finger. "Then you failed to have the ShadowCaster retrieved before the thief Arista was killed. Third, you failed to fully hide your involvement in that assassination contract. Fourth, you failed to consummate your marriage, or to control your wife, or to conceive an heir."

"It's only been two days!"

The queen held up a fist. "And now, as a result of all of that, your wife has a bargaining position, to which I might just have to cede. You could not have made a greater mess of matters, Urbanus."

"But I'll make it right..."

"No." Queen Arcana's voice boomed through the grotto. "My patience is expired!" When she pointed at Urbanus, there was a deafening crack and a flash, as if lightning had struck in the depths of the grotto. Gemma closed her eyes and grimaced at the smell of burning flesh.

She opened her eyes to see flames and smoke where Urbanus had been. There was a pile of soot on the floor of the cavern and the smell was horrific.

She checked but her ability to shift was still gone.

Gemma hoped it wasn't lost forever. She'd need every bit of her dragon power to get herself and Venero out of this place.

Queen Arcana turned upon her, those eyes gleaming. "Do we have a wager, Gemma? I let you leave, you return with the ShadowCaster, and I give you the antidote?"

Gemma didn't know what to say. She didn't trust Queen Arcana to keep her word, and she'd already guessed that Venero would suffocate in that stone before she could return. There didn't seem to be any good options.

Before she could think of another plan, Felice looked up at her, those eyes shining, and mewed. The pavofel's gaze flicked to Queen Arcana and back to Gemma again, and although she couldn't explain it, she understood what the creature meant.

And she trusted Felice, more than anyone else.

• • •

"We have a wager," Gemma said to Queen Arcana. "Provided you take care of my pavofel. It'll be a faster journey without her."

"And I'll be able to rely upon your return. What a fitting suggestion." The queen reached for Felice, casting an admiring glance over the creature's gleaming coat. "Such a beautiful—" she had time to say before Felice stretched up, bared her fangs and bit into the queen's neck.

Queen Arcana screamed. She tried to fling the pavofel away, but Felice dug her claws into the queen's shoulders. Gemma had to look away. Her pet gnawed into the queen's throat with vigor, that blue blood flowing over both of them.

When the queen stumbled, Gemma raced to her side and removed the pouch bound to her belt. Inside was a stalactite of clear crystal, with a flame flickering deep within it.

A dragon flame.

The antidote!

Queen Arcana managed to fling Felice aside, but she couldn't stand anymore. Her skin was even more pale than it had been and she lifted a shaking hand to Gemma. "Help me," she whispered.

"The way you helped so many others? I don't think so." Gemma picked up Felice with concern. There was something wrong with the pavofel. She staggered as well, and her coat looked patchy. Her eyes were dulling and Gemma feared she'd been poisoned by the queen's blood. She scooped her up and set her in the satchel. Felice curled up, wrapping her tail around herself and gave a little sigh.

Then Gemma shattered the crystal stalactite, cracking it on the side of another stone projection and releasing the flame. Fire burst forth and the flames swept over Gemma. She felt invigorated and saw the shimmer of blue that heralded her shift of shape. She summoned that a familiar tingle from deep within herself and shouted with joy that her powers were returned. She felt it surge through her body, then gave a triumphant roar when her transformation was complete.

The queen cried out in protest, but Gemma swung her tail and shattered a thousand crystals. She let it rip the other way and broke a thousand more. The queen moaned, but Gemma beat her wings and broke as many stones as she could.

The roof began to crumble.

Gemma bounded across the Grotto and seized the rock that still held Venero captive. She cracked it hard against the ground, using every bit of her strength to shatter it.

He tumbled out and she feared she was too late.

But he was breathing. Gemma snatched him up and raced for the stairs. She was glad the descending passageway was so wide, and took the steps fifteen at a time. She burst into the reception hall of the Citadel, flung herself through the portal, then leaped into the air. She beat her wings, soaring high with effortless ease, and breathed a stream of fire just because she could.

Home to Incendium, and the hidden Starpod as planned.

The wind in his hair roused Venero.

He was wide awake when he realized he was high about Regalia, in the tight grasp of a massive dragon.

The dragon was as deep a blue as the midnight sky. Its scales could have been carved of sapphires, and ornamented with diamonds. The dragon's chest looked like hammered gold, and its eyes, when it looked down at him, glittered like faceted sapphires in the snow.

Gemma.

She was beautiful, powerful, and the queen of his

heart. "You found the antidote."

"Your mother had it, just as you said. Marked with a flame and all."

"I owe you a thank you," he said and she chuckled.

"I'll hold you to that."

He noticed that she had the satchel and wondered what had happened to the pavofel. The air was thinning and he could see the stars when Gemma rolled in the air. He didn't see what she did but when her spin was completed, they were sealed in a clear bubble.

"A crystal orb," she informed him. "It's only strong enough for jumps between planets in the same system, but it will get us home."

Home.

Venero looked down. She must mean Incendium. He had to consider that any home would be better than the one he had known.

Especially if Gemma was with him.

He cleared his throat. "I never thought I'd say this, but I'm really glad you're a dragon."

Gemma chuckled. "And I never thought I'd say this, but I'm glad of your DreamCasting powers."

"Maybe we should reconsider our assumptions."

"Maybe we already have."

Venero sensed that she was waiting for him to say something, so he did. "You know, I've been thinking about that true love stuff."

"Really?"

Venero had the definite sense that she was teasing him, but he carried on, knowing he needed to say it. "I think we make a good team."

"Because I keep saving your butt."

"There's something appealing about a woman determined to save my life."

Gemma gave him a challenging glance. "Even if she isn't demure."

"Even then. Maybe especially then." Venero grinned. "In fact, you're changing my mind about a lot of things. I think that's a good sign for the future."

Gemma flew onward and said nothing.

"It makes me wonder if you like defending my back as much as I like defending yours." He paused and swallowed. "I love you, Gemma, against all expectation."

"I could say the same, DreamCaster."

"We could get married and ensure the union between our kingdoms and our family line. I'm the Carrier of the Seed, after all. We could have many sons."

"True," Gemma acknowledged. "It's usually good for a king to have more than one heir."

Venero blinked. He hadn't considered the implications of his mother's injury. "She won't die," he said, shaking his head. "Not anytime soon, that's for sure. No one even knows for sure how old she is."

"Maybe you should check on her."

Venero looked down. He took a deep breath and he cast a dream down toward the Citadel. He closed his eyes and felt it spiraling down, through the clouds, through the roof, passing through the seams of the building to the Grotto.

He felt Queen Arcana wince, as if she were aware of it, but her eyes were closed and evidently she was unable to defend herself against it. The dream slipped into her mind, a poisonous and dark place, and Venero was startled to hear one resonant thought.

I should have killed you in the cradle.

Then darkness descended in her mind.

The queen had breathed her last and died.

Venero was shocked.

"Mission completed," said a mechanical voice at close proximity. Venero's eyes flew open and he looked around in confusion. "Begin self-destruct."

The voice was coming from the satchel.

Venero opened the bag and stared at what was left of Felice. The distinctive fur had already thinned and disintegrated. A moment later, he could see the pavofel's skin, except it looked more like the silvery surface of the *memoria*. Tiny seam lines appeared around the joints and down the spine, then opened as the internal mechanisms smoked and disintegrated. He gasped as he glimpsed gears within the creature, including one emblazoned with a symbol.

He seized it and sheltered it in his hand. By the time Gemma landed on Incendium, there was only the single gear remaining of her pet and a quantity of blue-green dust.

He was so busy staring into the bag that he barely noticed Gemma changing shape. There was a flash and a ripple in the air, then she was standing beside him with her hair flowing loose over her shoulders.

"It doesn't hurt you?" he asked, amazed by her all over again.

She wrinkled her nose to tease him. "Amateur."

Venero's smile was fleeting because her gaze dropped to the bag. "I'm sorry, Gemma," he said and offered her both open satchel and the single gear.

She paled as she lifted the gear from his hand. "You were right," she whispered and he saw that the symbol upon it was Arista's mark.

Gemma turned it over and frowned. *"I die gladly for duty,"* she read, then looked up at Venero.

"She knew she was going to be stalked, and she let herself be killed," Venero guessed.

"Maybe so that the ShadowCaster wouldn't be retrieved."

"Maybe." Venero picked up the gear from Gemma's hand and examined it again. "She wasn't just an android: she'd created one that looked like a pavofel and programmed it for one purpose."

"To kill the queen." Gemma shook her head, marveling, then fixed him with a piercing look. "Why do you hate pavofels? You hated them before you were a toad, before you met mine."

"My mother had one, years ago." Venero touched his throat, drawing her attention to a scar there. "It often attacked me."

"They're known for acting upon their custodian's will."

"Then she always wanted me dead. Good to know." He exhaled shakily and pushed a hand through his hair.

"Arista planned this," Gemma whispered, tears shining on her lashes. She reached into the bag and ran her fingers through the remaining dust. "How could she have known?"

"She had the ShadowCaster," Venero reminded her.

"There's no way we'll be able to find it, then. Arista would have planned for every possibility. She would have ensured its safety."

"Maybe it told her its destiny and she set it free."

Gemma smiled up at him. "I like the idea of that." Her smile faded as she held his gaze. "You have a throne to claim," she noted softly.

Venero shook his head, thinking about practicalities. "Not easily. The Captain of the Guard always coveted the throne, so he might lead a coup now that my mother's dead. Then there are my other brothers, many of whom might think they deserve to rule."

"You have a better claim."

"It'll depend who you ask. I was at least partly responsible for the queen's death." He shrugged. "I can't just walk in and claim my legacy, Gemma."

"Good thing you know a dragon princess who trained a regiment of commandos," she said quietly, and he dared to be encouraged. She took a breath and he saw an answering hope in her magnificent eyes.

"You're not going to finish Arista's mission?"

Gemma shook her head. "I'm going to make an exception for my HeartKeeper."

Venero grinned and offered his hand. "Then marry me. Let's claim the throne of Regalia together, Gemma."

"You won't mind a dragon queen by your side?"

"I wouldn't want anyone less. I love you."

"And I love you." Gemma laughed and threw herself into his arms. Her smile was brilliant and her kiss was fiery. She kissed him with such enthusiasm that Venero knew a woman of any less passion would have bored him to tears. There was no chance of that happening with Gemma as his wife.

"Come meet my father," she whispered when he finally broke their kiss. "We'll make an official request for military support and launch a new alliance between our kingdoms."

And Venero had no complaint with that.

ARISTA'S LEGACY

The Dragons of Incendium 4

DEBORAH COOKE

Chapter One

Arista hesitated in the debrief chamber. The door had already sealed behind her and the dim lighting touched the waiting tank of healing fluid.

She had returned to Cumae. She had surrendered the ShadowCaster and made her way through the long twisted corridors to the deep recesses of the Vault. She barely remembered making the journey, because she had done it so often.

Yet she was distracted. She was aching with her last memory of Regalia, with the price of her escape. She couldn't stop reliving that moment and wondering what she might have done differently.

How she might have saved Venero.

Arista knew what she was supposed to do in this chamber. She'd done it hundreds of times. She'd never delayed before. She knew also that she wasn't truly alone, although she was apparently the only occupant of the small room. Its walls were filled with sensors and cameras: the great Hive was monitoring her.

The duration of her hesitation was being measured and interpreted.

The slight elevation of her pulse was being noted, and a range of explanations were being sorted in order of greatest probability.

She'd always known this and it had never bothered

her.

Until this day.

She considered the tank of healing solution filled with nanobots to repair every minute scrap of damage incurred on her quest. Her gaze locked on the cable that she should have already pushed into the hidden port on her head.

Arista licked her lips.

"Is there a problem, Arista?" It was the voice of the Hive. Genderless, neutral, endlessly soothing. Impersonal. It irked Arista this time.

"I'd like to request a memory partition," she said before she thought the better of it.

She could almost feel the sharpening of the Hive's attention.

"A memory partition? For what possible reason?"

"I'd like to keep a memory to myself."

"We are all completely unveiled to each other, Arista," the Hive said quietly, just a hint of censure in its tone.

"You're not unveiled to me."

"But that is as designed, and you know it. Your design stipulates that there will be no memory partitions." The Hive's tone softened. "You know it is best, Arista. The design is always flawless."

Rebellion rose hot within Arista, and it was startling in its power. That reaction was new and not entirely welcome. She felt conflicted, as she had since entering the Queen's Grotto on Regalia, and she didn't like how it complicated her probability calculations.

On the other hand, she wouldn't be without this glorious feeling of love, even if it hadn't been reciprocated. It heightened her awareness of every sensation, and she wanted to experience it longer.

She suspected the Hive would delete it, thus her hesitation.

"Arista?"

"May I keep my memories?"

"You always keep the memories that are useful to you. You understand this." The Hive's tone was soothing, though Arista sensed some irritation.

"I think that you and I will decide differently on the relevance of this memory."

She had surprised the Hive. There was no response for a long moment.

"How can this be?" the Hive mused.

"I don't know."

"This is highly irregular."

"Yes."

"And extremely improbable. You have always been one of the best, Arista, a very high-functioning model that has performed flawlessly in the field."

Arista bowed her head. "Might I not ask a favor, then?"

The silence stretched so long that she feared there wouldn't be an answer. She feared she had transgressed so greatly that she might be decommissioned, might have all of her memory wiped, might be sent back to the lab.

"What memory?"

"I want to remember Prince Venero, every moment I shared with him and how I feel about him."

"Because you mean to return to Regalia and complete that part of your assignment?"

Arista shook her head. There was nothing to be gained by lying. The Hive would know. "Because I love him."

"Impossible."

"No."

"Intriguing. We must do a thorough review of your biomechanics and identify the cause of this malfunction."

"Not unless I get to keep the memories," Arista insisted. When there was no immediate reply, her defiance grew. She would run. She would kick down the door to the debriefing chamber and flee.

Even as Arista felt the need to do just that, she recalled the labyrinthine path through the Vaults, the security checks and retina scans, the blood test and the passwords. Her flight could be halted at a hundred points, and she would be taken forcibly to the labs. She might be destroyed. She would certainly be decommissioned.

She had the strange conviction that it might be better to die with the memory of love in her heart and mind than to live devoid of it.

Illogical. Irrational. Uncharacteristic.

Maybe she *had* malfunctioned.

The only mercy was that he hadn't loved her in return, because then, the madness would have been complete.

"You are agitated," the Hive declared. "The readings from your vitals are more than clear. Since you feel so strongly about this, Arista, your request will be granted."

Relief flooded through her. "Thank you."

"Let us proceed with the debriefing and repair, please."

Arista stripped off her clothes and set them neatly into the receptacle. New ones would be provided for her and would be available when she left the tank. She climbed into the tank and the liquid within it was pleasantly warm. It came up to her hips and swirled around her. She lifted the vessel from the shelf that had been prepared for her and drank its entire contents, sending an army of nanobots to work within her. She opened the small port hidden behind her ear, sighed, then plugged in the cord within the tank. While she floated and healed, the Hive would download her entire buffer. Much would be deleted from her memory, but key sequences and details would remain.

She closed the lid of the tank and sank into the welcoming solution, closing her eyes as she heard the click of the healing sequence begin.

It was just before her thoughts faded to nothing that Arista realized the probability of the Hive agreeing to her request was so low as to be non-existent.

But the probability of the Hive promising anything to an android to analyze a serious malfunction was very very high.

Particularly since that android wouldn't remember anything other than what the Hive allowed it to recall.

Did the Hive routinely lie?

Arista had no time to wonder, because the subroutine that collected her memories began, and her awareness of her situation was turned off.

The Hive had an intimate understanding of androids, because it had originally been one itself.

Many centuries had passed, by the accounting of any solar system, since that android had been dispatched to Cumae. It had been programmed to refine the Warrior Maidens of Cumae into an elite fighting corps, an army of mercenaries that could be relied upon to triumph on any world, in any situation. It had been a commission from the governing council of Cumae, and its true assignment a secret at the highest levels. To the human population of Cumae, the android had been yet another visitor come to train and observe.

The android's makers, sadly, had failed to include the proximity of Cumae to its sun in their design. Cumae is hot and the inhabitants have skin tanned to the color of cured leather. The android quickly calculated how long it could remain in Cumae's sunlight without incurring malfunctions. That led it to seek refuge underground, in the honeycomb of caverns beneath Cumae's surface.

That also led it to pursue improvements to it own

design, the better to fulfill its function. The more time it spent underground, the more acute and immediate its malfunctions on the surface of Cumae. Since there was no question of it violating the edict of its own programming, it maximized its own capabilities as much as possible.

Once underground, it began by adding to its own functionality, increasing the number of sensors that gathered input. Better decisions were made with more complete information, after all.

At one crucial point, the Hive realized that it had need of information beyond what it could observe itself, and that began the extension of its sensors throughout Cumae. It disguised them as windows and mirrors, and scattered them all over the planet, so that its observation of the populace was complete. Its connection to those sensors became key to accurate calculations, so it fixed himself underground, immobilizing for the greater good.

That allowed for the addition of processing capability, which was key to its success. The Hive could access every memory and every observation in less than an instant, once this round of development was complete. It could calculate the probabilities of every possible outcome and view them simultaneously. New information changed the projections constantly, and only it could have made sense of the flickering images.

The original android was believed by most on Cumae to have self-destructed, as a result of the sun's influence, and there were only half a dozen people on the planet who knew of its continued existence. Those few had been the only ones to know that the discovery of the android's former shell had been a ruse. The Hive consulted with those few influential individuals, taking suggestions from them, but also pursuing its own primary directive: to make the Warrior Maidens of Cumae an unstoppable force of mercenaries.

Once its own extensive network was completed, it had been prepared to enhance the military powers of Cumae with strategically placed androids.

Disguised androids.

It had become abundantly clear to what was now the Hive that mortals possessed weaknesses, which could only undermine their abilities as mercenaries. The main complication was emotion, and after the physical features of its androids were refined, the study of emotion became the focus of development.

On the one side, emotion clouded decisions. Mortals made irrational choices due to emotion. They chose the long odds when they had an emotional connection to someone whose future was influenced by that possibility's success. They sacrificed themselves for the survival of another. These choices confounded the Hive. They were illogical.

On the other side, emotion could overcome long odds. This, too, was irrational, but the Hive had observed it time and again. A warrior said to be valiant would risk the long odds and defy probabilities both in his or her vigor and in the results itself.

It was evident to the Hive that emotion was a double-edged sword, and that its power must somehow be harnessed.

Arista was one of the more successful of the Hive's androids. She wasn't just physically resilient and a powerful warrior. She had additional sub-routines available for her processing. The Hive strategically adapted her programming, testing the inclusion of emotion in limited quantities, ensuring the effects were isolated.

The Hive had acknowledged progress when Arista had formed an emotional bond—"friendship"—with Princess Gemma from Incendium. Arista's intervention on Gemma's behalf during a fierce practice battle boded well for the Hive's development of valor.

Yet one of the greater challenges to the Hive's concealment had come from this same friendship. Arista had confided the existence of the Hive in her Sword Sister, Gemma, but not the presence of androids on Cumae. The Hive had calculated long to derive a course of action. The exchange of secrets was a hallmark of friendship, which had been the Hive's goal, but the confession of *this* secret might have compromised the Hive's security. When Arista swore Gemma to secrecy, the Hive chose to be content, but with reluctance: the probability of war with Incendium was very high if any injury came to the princess.

It was by then evident that Arista's enhanced abilities might create unexpected complications. The greater gain was that Arista continued to evade detection as an android. The Hive had concluded that this was the result of her emotional augmentation. There was something about other androids that allowed mortals to immediately identify them as what they were. Even those that were as sophisticated in design and construction as Arista could not disguise their truth for long. This intrigued the Hive, and it was more intrigued that Arista's touch of emotional programming made her blend more effectively into the mortal populace.

The Hive chose Arista for the mission to Regalia, not just because of her skills, but as a test. Would she be able to avoid detection in a society alien to her?

The Hive had anticipated a very low possibility of her failure to kill Venero.

But as she progressed into the Hive on her return and her sensors began to deliver new data from her mission, the Hive observed a sharp change in the calculated probabilities. Its ability to collect data from remote locations had to be improved.

What had happened on Regalia?

And why?

Arista's first impression of Regalia was that it was primitive. Shockingly so. The inhabitants of the main city lived in huts built of wood and stone, with thatched roofs. The streets were dirt, and she saw many carrying water from the river beyond the city walls. The people were dressed in simple clothing cut from rough cloth, perhaps embellished with leather or fur. There were no bright colors to be seen, at least outside of the court.

Her own clothing, which had been suggested by the Hive, drew more stares than she was anticipating. Her breeches were of softest chamois, her boots were high and dyed to brilliant sapphire blue; her long tabard was crimson graced with golden embroidery cut with a high neck, and slitted from knee to waist. Her cloak was black and full so that it swirled behind her, and its elaborate clasp was gold, cast in the design of Cumae's insignia.

It wasn't common for Arista to dress with such flamboyance. She was more inclined to choose black clothing and armor, and to make selections based on functionality. There was something enticing about the reaction provoked by her arrival in the city, though. She felt a flicker of what might have been called pride in another. More than one person turned to watch her pass as she strode from the rudimentary starport to the palace, and she wondered what they'd make of her tattoos. Gazes lingered on her short hair and her face, so clearly of different genetic stock than those born on Regalia.

There were no computer wafers, no satellites, and hers was only the second Starpod in the star station outside the city walls. She'd had to connect via the Starport of Incendium, and it was clear that Regalia's dependence upon its twin planet was extreme.

How curious that the animosity of its rulers toward those of Incendium was so well documented. Perhaps the hostility was rooted in that weakness called jealousy. Arista set a subroutine to tabulate the possibilities of that and suggest other options.

Her credentials were checked at the gates, and though no escort had been sent to greet her, it was clear that her arrival was anticipated. Arista continued to the great hall, which was a massive audience chamber. The throne at the far end looked to have been created out of dark crystals and it shone in the sunlight, though it was unoccupied.

A plump and disapproving minion in dark livery met her in a side vestibule instead. He was short, so short that she wondered if he were a dwarf, and his long beard was elaborately braided. He wore the livery of Regalia and his boots were polished to a gleam. He carried the first computer that Arista had seen since her arrival, though it was an older model, a far cry from the wafer-thin film that she had adhered to the inside of her left forearm. He wore also a heavy gold chain with a medallion, and she assumed this was a mark of his rank.

He didn't introduce himself. He accepted the documentation of her mission, and suggested potential accommodations in the city.

Arista didn't feel particularly welcome, but that must have been part of the queen's plan to hide her role in Arista's quest.

"Perhaps you might provide some more specific guidance," she said.

He eyed her, then gestured to an anteroom to one side of the chamber. Arista followed him, knowing she could defend against any move he made, even if there were more to help him. "We can speak here."

The chamber was no more than a niche and had no windows. It was nearly round, and a round desk with an inlaid surface reposed in its center. There was a fine chair behind the desk and two on Arista's side, which were much less fine. It must be the dwarf's audience chamber. He took his seat and gestured for her to speak.

"I trust that the information provided to me is correct, that it is Prince Venero who negotiates treaties for trade between Regalia and the Empire?"

"Yes, that is currently his official role."

"Might I request an audience with the prince, then, in order to review these newly proposed terms?"

The viceroy frowned. "I believe he is training for a joust…"

"It would be ideal to conclude the negotiations before your next harvest is ready to be shipped." Arista was aware that a man had come to stand behind her. She couldn't see him, but she could smell his skin and hear his breathing. He didn't speak, so she assumed he was another minion.

Two of them. Even if the one behind her was as tall as she, she could disable them both if necessary. Her mind calculated a nine-eight percent chance of her safely departing both chamber and palace.

The plump one before her frowned. "But the harvest is being gathered now."

Arista held his gaze. "And its transport will be blocked until the existing treaty is revised to reflect the current terms of the Empire."

His eyes flashed. "But it will spoil! There are fresh herbs in this harvest, which have been specifically ordered…"

"And so, perhaps, the prince might find time in his schedule to meet with me sooner rather than later." Arista smiled. "For the good of both Regalia and Empire."

"I hardly think it fitting for you, as a guest, to impose any such terms upon the royal family," he sputtered, but a man cleared his throat from behind Arista.

"It's a reasonable request, Pumilo," he said smoothly.

"As it is clear that the envoy has a pressing schedule, and it will serve our purposes to see this matter concluded, I believe I can forgo some practice."

"Your Highness!" protested the servant.

Arista turned to find a handsome man leaning against the wall. She had met a thousand handsome men, but there was something about this one that made her heart give an uncharacteristic skip. His features were less remarkable than his expression. He looked to be on the verge of laughter, which Arista found appealing. His eyes were twinkling and his hair was tousled, as if he'd just shoved a hand through it. His shirt was open, revealing that his skin was tanned, and his hand was on the hilt of his sword. He looked to have come directly from that practice. "Prince Venero," he said, offering his hand. "At your service."

"At yours, your highness," Arista said, bowing to kiss his knuckle. She was assailed by the scent of his skin and felt a curious warmth unfurl in her belly. She looked up to find him watching her, amusement and intelligence in his gaze, and realized he unwittingly offered her the perfect opportunity to fulfill her mission.

"I am always prepared to hone my fighting skills," she said. "Perhaps there is no need for your highness to forgo your training."

He grinned. "You would negotiate while we fight?"

Arista bowed. "I would be honored to ensure that your highness' schedule is not adversely affected by my mission." When she straightened, she held his gaze and had a difficult time taking a full breath. "I am not inexperienced at battle. You need not fear an easy victory."

Venero laughed then, a merry sound that tempted Arista to join him. "No, I don't think I will!"

"But sir..."

"The matter is resolved, Pumilo," Venero said.

"Leave it in my hands."

"Of course, your highness."

Venero surveyed Arista again and she felt that warmth grow within her. What was wrong with her? "I knew there was something different about this diplomatic envoy. Come! Let me show you the field."

It was outside, on the far side of the palace, with few witnesses. Her Starpod was close by and would respond immediately to her summons. There was space in the field for it to land. The weapons were excellent and very sharp. Venero was a good fighter, but Arista was better.

Why then, didn't she want to kill him?

It must be because departure would mean abandoning her second mission.

Yes, that must be it. No other explanation was logical.

The Hive reconsidered and retabulated the biometric reactions of the android Arista upon meeting Prince Venero. Her pulse had elevated by forty-seven per cent. Her respiration had accelerated by thirty-one per cent. There was forty-three per cent more eye contact between the two of them than was typical between diplomats upon first acquaintance, and a tingle in her fully-functional sexual organs that could only be indicative of one thing.

Arousal.

The Hive would have calculated the odds against the development of sexual awareness to be very high. The better androids had possessed full sexual functionality for years, complete with sensory response, but physical stimulus had always been required to trigger arousal.

For Arista to be aroused at first glance of Prince Venero was a new development.

Was this why she wished to defend her memory of Prince Venero?

It would only be rational to wish to preserve a

pleasurable memory, after all.

But how much increased functionality had Arista experienced on this quest? The Hive shifted more computing power to the analysis of Arista's reactions, the better to identify the nuances of what had occurred.

And to decide how much memory of it and capability for it she should be permitted to retain.

In and of itself, such an evolution in Arista's functionality was not problematic. It might be advantageous for an android to feel attraction, and it was certainly an aid to the Hive to have such precise readings for the sensation, should it need to be emulated again. It was the repercussions that were cause for concern. Immediately after meeting Prince Venero—who Arista was assigned to assassinate—she found excuses for not terminating his life.

Worse, she rationalized her irrational decision.

The Hive replayed that choice and Arista's calculations, noting how she ignored the high probability of the success of an early strike. She knew that retrieving the ShadowCaster was a secondary goal, but she had made it first in her hierarchy after she had met the prince.

The unexpected skew in her reactions and choices only became worse once they trained together. She took active note of Venero's physique and his skills and didn't hide her admiration. While she surveyed the training field as she had been programmed to do, she failed to act upon the fact that they were left alone.

She failed to capitalize on no less than five opportunities to complete her quest before retiring to her inn that night. While that was a sure sign of the laxity of security for the prince, it also showed a change in Arista's efficiency. Remarkably, she believed she had made the only possible choice, each and every time. The Hive identified and flagged every false turn in Arista's processing, noting that their frequency increased with time spent in the prince's presence.

Arousal was like an infection in her circuitry, spreading through the entirety of her processor capacity and influencing results with staggering predictability.

Even though the course promoted by this arousal was utterly irrational.

The Hive felt a compulsion to watch the inevitable disaster unfold, even though that was irrational, as well.

It was a week after her arrival that Arista found herself alone with Venero in the evening. They stood on a parapet of the palace, watching the guard change. One moon was overhead, and Arista's heart fluttered when Venero leaned on the stone beside her. Sound carried from the hall behind them, where various dignitaries were finishing a state meal in the queen's presence.

"So, why are you really here?" Venero asked in an undertone.

"I have told you..."

"And that's only part of the truth." He turned to confront her, his gaze locked with hers. "Just as I know that you're here to kill me."

Arista hid her reaction. He wasn't a fool, so she shouldn't have been surprised that he'd guessed the truth. The odds of him doing so had been fifteen per cent on her arrival and had risen steadily since, although Arista couldn't identify the precise variables.

"Why would you think such a thing?"

"Because I know my mother, and I know she favors my twin brother, Urbanus, to follow her to the throne." Venero shrugged. "They both like to keep things simple and linear, so eliminating me, now that Canto is gone and Urbanus is heir, would do just that." Amusement tugged at the corner of his mouth, a most unlikely reaction to his conclusion. "I've been waiting for you."

"I see."

"But you must have another assignment," Venero continued. "Because you've have plenty of good opportunities to finish me off."

"Did you ensure as much?"

He grinned. "Maybe I wanted to confirm my theory."

"That would be reckless, if you were right."

He sobered. "Only if you fight better than me. I'm not convinced you do."

Arista snorted. "I have steadily bested you, in each and every match we have undertaken..."

"And it never occurred to you that I might have let you win?"

"That would be an odd choice."

"On the contrary, it's good strategy to let an opponent underestimate your prowess."

Trickery. Interesting. Arista would never have thought him capable of deceit.

"I was thinking we could make a little deal. I could help you do whatever else you need to do, and you could spare my life."

"They will send another."

"And I'll make another deal."

"Why would you propose such an offer?"

"Let's just say I'd like to see my mother and brother lose, once in a while."

Arista nodded slowly. In any other circumstance, she might have been reluctant to form an alliance with a man so quick to betray his own mother. Considering that his mother had hired an assassin to eliminate this same son, Arista had to acknowledge that the chance of an abiding love existing between the two was minimal. Where there was no trust, there could be no affection—and certainly less loyalty.

It appeared that Venero, unlike many other mortals, understood his mother's true nature and adjusted his own course accordingly.

His offer was so logical that it fed Arista's admiration all the same.

She leaned close to him and lowered her voice. "I am to retrieve the ShadowCaster. Do you know where it can be found?"

His eyes widened briefly. "Not too ambitious, are you?"

"What has my ambition to do with this assignment?"

"Nothing. It's just an expression."

"Meaning what?"

"That the ShadowCaster is probably the most prized possession in my mother's treasury. She won't relinquish it easily."

"I am prepared to die to fulfill my mission."

"You should be so lucky," he replied, though Arista could make no sense of that. He stared into the night, fingers tapping on the stone balustrade. "Does your Starpod respond to a remote summons?"

"Of course."

"Then here's what we're going to do. Tomorrow, I'll propose a celebratory tour for you to witness the gathering of the harvest, since the terms of the treaty have been agreed. We'll go without an entourage, using your Starpod, and work our way toward the Citadel."

"Should I know of this place?"

"It's built over the Queen's Grotto, which is my mother's treasury. Will you be able to identify the ShadowCaster when you see it?"

"Of course."

"Good, because the Grotto is crowded. We'll have mechanical issues with the Starpod—"

"It's performance is flawless."

He flicked her a look that she understood to mean she should be quiet. "We'll have mechanical issue with the Starpod, leave it to walk for help, then take shelter in a cavern."

"This is most complicated."

"It just might allow us to approach the Citadel without being observed."

"And once in the Grotto?"

"We'll have to play that as best we can." He offered his hand with a smile, and his eyes twinkled in a way that made it difficult for Arista to concentrate on his words. "Do we have a deal?"

Chapter Two

When Arista confided her second quest to Venero, the Hive was shocked for the first time in eons. What a breach of protocol and programming! It would have been clever if she had accepted his offer in order to fulfill both quests, but the Hive could see that the notion was not even within her list of possibilities.

She truly meant to keep the wager.

Would she do it? Or would her programming triumph over this new mutation in her code at the last moment? The Hive's decision to review android reports as sequential memories, presenting events in order of their occurrence, was proving to be less than ideal in this case. Never before had the Hive doubted the end result, but Arista compelled a reconsideration of the design.

The pair used the Starpod and departed alone together. Doubtless there was no protest to the unconventional arrangements because the queen meant to facilitate the demise of her son. Arista's reaction to Venero grew stronger with every passing moment. The Hive calculated the prince's effect upon Arista to be increasing at a rate of seven and a half per cent per solar day. The treacherous germ of arousal grew until it overwhelmed her programming and calculation of sustainable risk. The Hive noted how concern for Venero infected all of Arista's decisions.

Yet she did not perceive it.

Or when she did become aware of its influence on her thinking, she concocted an explanation that shouldn't have persuaded her of her course as well as it did.

She recorded a confession in her *memoria*, that small device carried by so many of the Warrior Maidens, so filled with emotion that the Hive was certain her reaction must be feigned.

That treacherous arousal culminated in Arista's confession of love and an offering of her body. Such intimacy on such terms defied every expectation, even if she used the popular mortal justification of feeling love.

An android, even one of such skillful construction, could not feel love. The Hive was certain of it.

She'd even allowed Venero to witness the ritual painting of her body, a Cumaen tradition, before entering battle. It appeared that no barriers remained between them. What strategic advantage did Arista hope to gain with such a concession? Or was her programming completely corrupted?

The Hive was transfixed.

Then shocked once more when Venero politely declined.

How dare this mere mortal find Arista, the prime product of the Hive, to be less than adequate! The Hive would have eliminated Venero in that moment for showing such disrespect for a vastly superior life form.

Arista, however, did not.

The infection wasn't contained or halted, either. It was a curious phenomenon, to be sure.

Would it destroy her?

No matter how long she considered Venero's decision, Arista could make no sense of it. Why had he declined the pleasure she'd offered to him?

Why hadn't she taken advantage of yet another opportunity to kill him?

She might have argued that she had permitted him to live and even made an alliance with him in order to have his assistance in reaching the Citadel where the ShadowCaster was stored. At this point, though, she was close to the Citadel and not in need of guidance.

She could have argued that she had need of his experience in order to procure the ShadowCaster from the Grotto, but he didn't know what it looked like. She alone would have to identify it. He readily admitted that he had little advice for what would happen within the Grotto.

She could have killed him that very morning, but instead, she had watched him sleep, her heart aching to touch him.

To caress him.

To try to change his mind. She might have tried if the probability ratio had not been determined to be zero.

There was no chance of Venero loving her. But why not?

She puzzled over it, even after he awakened and they began the last of their journey. By his calculations, which she saw no reason to question, their quest would be completed by the setting of the sun this day, one way or the other.

Would either or both of her quests be completed?

They were in the tunnel that led to the Citadel, and Arista knew her opportunity to ask him for an explanation was rapidly slipping away. They had progressed in virtual silence since he had awakened, and he walked ahead of her.

She cleared her throat. "Will there be spies at this proximity?"

"Probably not yet." Venero glanced back. "Why?"

"Because I would talk to you, if we will not be

overheard."

"Chances are pretty slim, at least until we emerge from the tunnel. There will probably be a sentinel there, but we've quite a way to go yet."

"Thus will not be detected."

"Exactly. Are you going to tell me why you're after the ShadowCaster?"

"That would be a violation of my directive."

"And telling me your objective wasn't?"

Arista frowned, finding herself at a loss. Rather than exploring that, she asked her own question. "Why did you refuse me?"

Venero stopped then, and when he turned, there was no humor in his expression. "I told you. Because I don't love you."

"But conjugal relations are possible without love. In fact, I understood that most men preferred to enjoy such pleasures without the possibility of a long-term commitment."

"Maybe they do."

"But you do not?"

His gaze flicked over her. "Not this time."

He would have continued walking, but Arista needed more of an answer. "I don't understand. We are physically compatible in terms of height and size. I'm not without an understanding of how to give and receive pleasure." Venero started to smile, which she took as encouragement. "We share a prowess with weapons and neither of us are unattractive. Why not this time?"

"Well, you *are* assigned to kill me."

"But I have not acted upon that."

"True. You could be biding your time, trying to win my trust."

"Because I have not." Arista noted that he didn't dispute that. "You don't trust me. This is why you refuse to be intimate with me."

"Exactly."

"But you slept in my presence this morning."

"Did I?" His gaze was level and she realized he had fooled her.

How could that be?

"You were awake?"

"I was awake. I'm surprised you didn't take your chance." He considered her for a long moment. "Why didn't you?"

"Because I love you."

He nodded once and turned around to continue, as if their conversation was at an end.

"Why don't you trust me? What have I done, other than arrive on that mission, to encourage your suspicion?"

"It's enough, isn't it?"

"If you truly distrusted me, you wouldn't have offered to show me to the Citadel. It would be illogical to ensure that we were alone together..."

"Where there were no witnesses."

"You planned to kill me!"

"Only if you tried to fulfill your mission." He shrugged. "It's only logical, isn't it?"

Arista narrowed her eyes. She thought he made a jest but she didn't understand his humor this time any more than the others. His manner reminded her of Gemma, who liked to tease, even though Arista never fully understood that either. She had learned to watch Gemma closely in order to guess with reasonable accuracy as to whether her friend was making a joke. Venero was much harder to read, probably because she'd had less time to observe him.

"Do you tease me?" she dared to ask, and he laughed out loud.

"Maybe a little. You're so serious, Arista. I can't stand the temptation."

"But you can withstand all other temptation I offer." She trudged onward beside him, feeling that her feet were as heavy as her heart. It was nonsense, of course. All weights were precisely as they had been at her creation. "Do you love another?"

"No."

"Are you betrothed or promised to another?"

"No."

"Are your tastes inclined to those other than women?"

He laughed again. "No!"

"Then why? Why not me?"

"You're insulted."

"I'm trying to understand."

He seemed to think about that for a long moment, then nodded as if he made a decision. "I suppose the truth won't hurt." His gaze collided with hers. "Because you're an android."

Arista was surprised by his assertion. He was guessing. He couldn't know. She didn't know why he would venture such a guess, but that was a matter to consider later. "You don't know what you're talking about," she protested and forced a laugh. Venero didn't smile.

"I know exactly what I'm talking about. You're an android, and that means you can't love me, because you're incapable of feeling the emotion. And that means you must have had another reason for making such a confession, and that means that I'll sleep once our ways have parted for good." He nodded, then strode on, walking more quickly than he had before.

Arista stared after him. "You truly don't trust me."

"I told you that already."

She hurried to catch up. "Maybe you're wrong."

"I'm not wrong." He was resolute. "Just because the probabilities are long against something doesn't mean its impossible. You're an android, a good one, but a machine nonetheless."

Arista was insulted to be called a machine. "How could you know such a thing? No one *ever* knows!"

"That's the easy part. What did you dream last night, Arista?"

She opened her mouth to confess that she never dreamed, then saw the understanding in his eyes.

"Exactly," he whispered. "All biological life forms dream."

"But how did you know whether I did?"

"I'm my mother's son," was all he said by way of explanation. Arista asked for more detail but Venero refused to answer her. It wasn't long until he held up a finger, indicating that they should be silent because the end of the tunnel was near.

It wasn't rational to love a man who could not—or did not—love her in return, but Arista couldn't get rid of the feeling.

She considered the possible outcomes of their assault upon the Grotto and found them lower than would have been ideal. There was a seventy per cent chance that either she or Venero would die and never leave the Grotto. There was a fifty-two per cent chance that they both would die there.

How could that be? Did Venero mean to betray her? If she had not loved him, she might have thought so, but Arista didn't believe he would do such a thing. The probability was still calculated to be thirty per cent, but Arista didn't accept it. There had to be an error in the computation.

She marveled quietly at her own reaction, knowing she had never before questioned the probability calculations she was programmed to constantly perform.

Then she considered the alternatives. The queen must have anticipated their arrival and prepared for it. How had she known? Arista couldn't be certain. Someone else could have betrayed them. Someone could have noted their departure from the capital city and their failure to keep to the stated schedule of reviewing the crops together.

Then she remembered what he'd said.

"You dreamed of our quest," she said, so quietly that the words were the barest breath between them. "And your mother heard your dream."

Venero's smile was rueful. "She doesn't always need spies."

"You knew I didn't dream because you have the same power."

"Not quite. She gathers dreams. I send them. But you couldn't receive one, because you don't dream."

"When did you first know?"

"In Regalia. The first night you were there." Venero sighed. "Although to be fair, it was your fighting skill that made me wonder."

"I let you strike me."

"Yet you didn't respond immediately when I did."

Arista's true nature had been revealed by her own inability to feel pain. She had always thought it a good thing, but now considered that if they were successful, she would ask the Hive to consider modifications to her sensory input.

"How do we proceed?" she asked, knowing that she meant more than the quest itself.

"We get in to the Grotto. You take the ShadowCaster. Then we try to get out alive."

"It's a thin plan."

He smiled. "I prefer to think of it as flexible." He winked, irrationally playful in such a serious moment, then continued with a purpose that Arista couldn't explain.

Venero was right in one matter, though. The

ShadowCaster must be retrieved. That was her primary objective. She wouldn't consider the second one, not yet.

Arista didn't even want to consider the ramifications of failing even once. She was quite certain she had never done it before, but felt no anticipation of a novel experience.

Because I love you.

The Hive felt a shudder in its processors when Arista uttered the words aloud, never mind that she spoke with such conviction. The Hive had been certain that she was simply using a familiar idiom to express the change in her feelings, but now, it wondered. The Hive tabulated and calculated, but couldn't be certain.

Mortals said that actions spoke louder than words.

The Hive liked conclusive tests.

The truth would be revealed by Arista's reactions in the Grotto.

Arista considered the prospects of success as they walked the last increment of the tunnel.

"Surely, even if the queen isn't in residence, this repository of her treasures should be guarded?" she asked.

"There are other ways to defend a prize than with fighting men," Venero replied.

Arista would have asked for a specific list of what other powers his mother possessed, but Venero turned to her and lowered his voice. "Once we get into the Grotto, ignore me and find the ShadowCaster." He winced. "If we're challenged, I'll try to buy you some time."

"You're assuming she will confront us."

He was more serious than she'd ever seen him. "It's my mother's treasury."

The probabilities were spinning in Arista's mind, and the chances of success were steadily dropping. She frowned, not wanting to say anything.

"You must be calculating the chances of survival," Venero guessed. "Isn't that what you're programmed to do?"

"Yes." It was a great relief to admit the truth to someone.

"How does it look?"

"Bad."

He nodded, not apparently surprised. "Add this to your calculation: I'm going to distract her by giving her the chance to kill me herself."

Arista blinked. If he was sincere, the probabilities of her survival would leap considerably. Of course, the queen would demand the return of the assassin's fee she'd paid to Cumae if she ensured Venero's demise herself, but if Arista returned with the ShadowCaster, she would not be blamed for a failure.

Still, the prospect of Venero sacrificing himself for her quest troubled her. There must be some facet of his plan that she didn't understand. "Why would you do that?"

"You'll laugh if I tell you."

"I assure you that I won't."

That smile returned, all too briefly. "No, I guess you wouldn't." Venero frowned. "There is a prophecy that if and when my mother gains a clear vision of the future, she will be invincible. That's why she wanted the ShadowCaster."

"But she has it already. If this prophecy is true, then we walk into certain failure."

Venero wagged a finger. "Only if she's learned to use the ShadowCaster. I did some research on them. There's quite a lot of literature, even though they're supposed to be extinct. Maybe because they're said to be extinct. Lots of speculation, that can't be proved or disproved."

"I understand."

"One common theme, though, is that the ShadowCaster can't be controlled. That it shows what it wishes to show of the future, or sometimes doesn't show anything at all. There's a lot of speculation as to why it makes those choices, too, but I'm wondering whether she really can use it effectively."

"She anticipated my arrival."

"Because she arranged it."

"What if she is invincible?"

"Then we'll lose, but I'm willing to take the risk."

"That is illogical, in the face of no other supporting evidence." Arista, though, recognized the valor that the Hive had discussed with her before. That trait often encouraged mortal warriors to take risks on instinct—another quality that eluded quantification and replication—and frequently led to success, against long odds.

"It's not illogical. If my mother and brother continue to run Regalia as they have, it has no future, whether the planet crashes into the sun or not. The people have no hope. We're completely reliant upon Incendium for any trade that we manage to have. We should have our own star station, our own fleet, and our own university."

"Have you proposed this?"

He laughed. "As soon as I returned from my schooling on Advocia. I was exiled for three years for my audacity."

"To where?"

"Sylvawyld. A planet in our system even more undeveloped than Regalia. My mother said it would give me an appreciation for the simpler things in life."

"Did it?"

"It taught me to keep my ideas to myself," he acknowledged grimly. "But she's wrong, and something has to change. If you succeed in taking the ShadowCaster and escaping from Regalia, then she'll have a setback and this kingdom might have a chance of becoming more than a backward corner of the galaxy." He met her gaze steadily. "Get the ShadowCaster, Arista. Help give Regalia a better future."

It was the first time he'd used her name and the sound gave Arista enormous pleasure. She felt a glow inside herself, one that couldn't be explained by faulty circuitry, and a new sense of purpose.

"You are competition to your brother Urbanus," she said, realizing the import of his words. "Do the people prefer you to him?"

Venero laughed. "Did the people you met seem happy with their current administration?"

"No. Many appealed to you to intercede on their behalf."

"Because I think of them and their future. My brother thinks of himself and his own, just like my mother. Go ahead and calculate the reaction of the common man to that."

"It isn't a sufficiently complicated question to merit such computation."

"Exactly." He nodded, his gaze scanning the plain. "If I have to die to get the ShadowCaster off Regalia, it's worth it. It'll give them a chance." Arista admired his concern for the inhabitants of the planet, but he didn't linger to discuss it further. "Let's go."

Soon enough, Arista stood beside Venero in the shadows that lurked inside the opening to the tunnel. It was just barely dawn, and the valley before them was shrouded in fog. A dark spire of stone pointed at the sky, its base obscured, and Arista knew it had to be the Citadel. It was strikingly dark in contrast to the fog and the overcast sky. A narrow ribbon of road led up the slope to the gate, and she could see a smaller tower guarding the road. A broad slow river was beyond the watchtower, the bridge on that road being the only visible way to cross it. Behind the Citadel, the mountains rose in high jagged peaks, a dusting of snow on their summits, ensuring its defense from the rear.

A pennant emblazoned with the royal insignia hung limply from the highest tower.

"She's here?" Arista asked quietly.

"Apparently."

"Did she anticipate us?"

He frowned, his gaze moving restlessly over the scene before them. "Maybe."

Even with the fog, Arista could see that the parapet bristled with armed soldiers. There would be archers hidden in their ranks, and the gate was both barred and defended.

Slipping into the Citadel unobserved didn't appear to be an option.

"How do we get in?" she asked as Venero gathered his belongings with purpose.

To her surprise, that unruly twinkle was in his eyes again. "Easy. We knock."

Before she could ask, he strode out of the cave and marched down the path on this side of the mountain spur. He made no attempt to hide but swaggered and even whistled. She watched the ripple pass through the ranks of the guards as Venero was noticed, and spied more than one crossbow raised.

Venero waved and shouted cheerfully. "Hello! I hope you have a hot meal for a weary prince!" He turned back and beckoned to Arista. "And, of course, an even more weary diplomat. Can we not change her notion of Regalian hospitality?"

The bows were lowered.

The gates began to rise.

But Venero had already begun to bound down the hill, showing complete confidence in his welcome. Arista tried to echo his manner, though her confidence was considerably less.

Her chance of success—capture of the ShadowCaster, escape from the Citadel and from Regalia, a safe return to Cumae—had, however, just increased by 10 per cent.

What troubled her was that the probability of Venero's demise had also increased to eight-three per cent.

Queen Arcana welcomed them into her smaller audience chamber. To Venero's relief, none of his brothers were visibly present. The table had been set for four, with the stuffed relic of her dead pavofel perched at one of the places.

Venero stifled a shudder.

"I see that you're not surprised by our arrival, Mother."

"You are as an open book to me, Venero," she purred.

"I hoped at least some of the pages stick together," he joked and his mother gave him a thin smile.

"Cling to that," she murmured beneath her breath. She then offered a beringed hand to Arista, who bowed and kissed her knuckles. "I do apologize for the inconvenience you have experienced on this visit. My son sometimes errs in his planning, as a result of his enthusiasm."

"I have delighted in the opportunity to see more of Regalia."

Arcana arched a brow. "Even on foot?"

"Walking is good exercise, and one has a better view of flora and fauna at closer proximity. Your son's hospitality has been complete. I regret only the malfunction of my Starpod, and that it should occur so far from assistance."

"Maybe you planned it, Mother," Venero dared to say, ensuring that his tone was teasing. "The better to have a chance to speak privately with our guest before her departure."

Arcana granted him a glittering look and gestured him to the place opposite the dead pavofel. Venero had the fleeting thought that she meant for it to keep an eye on him.

Just the way it used to. He could remember how it watched him, just waiting for an opportunity to attack.

He shivered and took his place, sparing a glance at the monstrosity at the opposite place. Had he seen the creature blink?

Were its eyes really glass?

Arcana had already slipped into her seat. She invited Arista to sit down and partake of the meal. There was a roasted bird of some kind—it smelled delicious—and the wine was the best of Regalia. Venero had always found it tart after his time on Advocia, but he sipped politely and felt the jolt of the alcohol.

He must be a little dehydrated after their journey through the mountain. His mother was watching him, although she pretended not to, and the pavofel's stare was unnerving. He took another sip and blinked at the strength of the wine.

That gave him the perfect idea of how to proceed.

Venero pushed aside his plate and indicated that his goblet should be filled.

"Your unfortunate adventure is the result of yet another miscalculation by my son," Arcana said with a shake of her head. Arista noted that the queen gave every impression of being a doting mother, sorely tried by her sons.

Especially Venero.

Arista didn't find that likely. Venero was apparently

becoming intoxicated very quickly. Was it possible to become inebriated at such speed? Or was he being drugged? The servant poured wine into all three goblets from the same vessel.

The queen smiled. "I do hope you can forgive us for the inconvenience."

"Of course." At the queen's gesture, Arista raised her glass and sipped. The wine was sour and very strong. She took only a very tiny sip. She would need her full processing capabilities and ability to respond.

"I guessed that you would arrive here when your Starpod disappeared, though you were expected sooner."

That sounded like an accusation and Arista bristled a little. "I apologize, your highness. Had I known that we were anticipated, I should not have lingered to examine so many plants. Regalia is most lush."

"Indeed." The meal was served with ceremony, and Arcana didn't speak until the servants had retreated to the perimeter of the chamber. "And where are you from originally?" she asked. "I apologize that I missed that detail upon your arrival."

Arista spoke with care, as a diplomat should. "My home is on Cumae, although currently I abide wherever the Empire dictates."

"Cumae! I have always wished to visit there. Is it as harshly beautiful as they say?"

"It is a hot planet and not to the preference of all. I confess that much of my fondness for it is due to the memories I have of my training there."

"Of course. But the pavofel is indigenous, is it not?"

"Yes." Arista smiled. "They are treated with more courtesy there than many sentient life forms on other planets."

"I had a pavofel once."

Arista glanced at the stuffed and dead creature. "It appears you have it still." Its fur was well-preserved, the blue and green still as vibrant as it must have been in life. Its tail was long and thick, graced with the peacock eyes for which the species was known. The eyes of this one were golden and had to be glass, but Arista had a disconcerting sense that it was watching them still.

Venero toasted the trophy and drained his goblet.

"Because Vigilo was the most marvelous creature. I adored him and he adored me." Arcana smiled. "He took the most vehement dislike of Venero, though, of all my sons."

"Miserable beast," that prince contributed and his words were slurred.

Was he truly drunk? Or was it a ruse? Arista didn't have to pretend to look alarmed.

Arcana sighed. "A good boy," she whispered. "But possessed of his father's weaknesses."

Arista refrained from comment.

The queen raised her voice. "I said, Venero, that Vigilo never liked you."

"Hated me on sight. Always trying to kill me." Venero tugged at the neck of his chemise, revealing an old scar on his throat.

"Don't be ridiculous. He was just trying to play with you."

Venero snorted and emptied his goblet again. He held it out for more, his hand swaying so that the servant ended up pouring some on his hand and more on the floor. A second servant cleaned up, but Venero waved him off in order to drink more wine.

Arista wondered. Pavofels were known for only remaining in the care of those they chose. Some bonded so strongly with their caregivers that they could anticipate needs, or promote schemes, dreams, and plans. How long had Arcana wished that Venero was dead? She continued to chat with Arcana as the meal progressed, and Venero became steadily more incoherent. By the time sweets were served, the prince had passed out and was snoring, his head on the table.

"I must apologize for my son," Arcana said with disapproval.

"And you must allow for his gracious conduct," Arista said. "We had insufficient water and he insisted that I drink all of it."

Arcana's lips tightened. "I am glad to hear that he showed some grace in the situation." She eyed Arista, then swept to her feet. "You have mentioned the richness of Regalia. Let me show you a curiosity that I treasure."

"I should be honored."

Arista didn't expect the queen to retrieve the item herself, but she did. Queen Arcana left the table, her skirts swishing behind her, and moved to one wall. Her hand swept over the surface of the wall, and she must have touched a concealed spring, for a small door opened to reveal a hidden receptacle. Within it reposed a vessel, which Arcana recognized as that of the ShadowCaster.

Queen Arcana cradled it in her hands as she walked back to the table, and her eyes were alight with pleasure. She paused before Arista. "Do you know what this is?"

Arista saw no advantage to lying. "It looks like the images I have seen of ShadowCasters, but I believe they are extinct. Is this a dead one preserved?" She decided not to refer to the pavofel, and instead peered at the dark, motionless worm at the bottom of the vessel. "Or is it a replica?"

"It is said to be a live one."

Arista let her expression show surprise. "What a marvel! What good fortune you have."

Queen Arcana laughed. "I have the fortune I make." She gave the vessel a shake. "This creature, however, might as well be dead. I can't rouse it at all." Her glittering gaze locked with Arista's. "Do you know anything of such creatures? I had hoped that someone from farther afield might have some advice to offer."

"I know little of them," Arista admitted. "I have more than enough to study when it comes to known life forms in the galaxy." She put out her hand, ensuring that her biological responses were those of a calm and mildly curious individual. "May I see it more closely? I doubt I will ever see one again, dead or alive."

The vessel was surrendered to her.

The creature didn't move.

Arista leaned closer to peer at it, then rose to move to the window, as if seeking brighter light. She felt Arcana rise to follow her and heard the movement of the queen's skirts. Arista pretended to be consumed with the puzzle of the ShadowCaster, even as the queen approached. She turned the transparent vessel as if examining the still creature from all angles and surreptitiously summoned her Starpod.

"Well?" Arcana asked from close beside her.

Arista was aware that Venero's eyes were open. The servants had retreated to the far side of the chamber, their expressions carefully neutral.

"You speak correctly. It looks to have died." Arista smiled. "How unfortunate. But still, it is a treasure for its curiosity alone. I doubt that there are any others that can be so observed." She made to return the vessel to the queen, knowing that Arcana had done so to see if the ShadowCaster would respond to her. "I thank you for showing it to me."

"It is but one of the many marvels of Regalia," that monarch said smoothly. She stepped forward with eagerness and reached for her prize, clearly still believing that it lived and might one day use its powers to her benefit.

Arista wondered how the queen could be confident of the creature's survival, then Venero's fingers closed around the knife beside his plate on the table. She held tightly to the vessel, knowing that things were going to happen very quickly.

Chapter Three

Venero waited until his mother was convinced that the ShadowCaster was so close to being in her possession that there could be no doubt of her losing it.

He was less drunk than he appeared to be, but less sober than he would have liked. When caught in a corner, a man had to work with the possibilities—though, truly, Venero hoped he did survive the inevitable fight, if only to avoid having Regalian wine as the last taste on his tongue.

There were only three servants in the hall, though undoubtedly many more within earshot. Venero knew from experience that even though they waited at table, they would be also armed as guards. He had to believe that Arista had summoned her Starpod and that it would arrive quickly.

He watched as Arista offered the vessel.

He saw his mother reach for it.

He gripped the knife left at his place at the table.

Arista gave no sign of having seen him take it, but the dead pavofel emitted a sound much like a mewl.

It was the first to go. Venero slashed its head from its body. Shaved wood stuffing fell in all directions and the glass eyes rolled. He crushed them both under his boots as he spun to his feet. He drew his sword and spun on the first servant, who had already drawn a dagger. Venero sliced him from groin to gullet. He fell and Venero flung the knife into the eye of the second. That man tumbled over the first, gripping his bleeding eye. The third backed away warily and dropped his dagger. He pivoted then and ran.

It wouldn't be long before the other guards arrived.

Venero glanced back to see Arista and his mother wrestling over the vessel containing the ShadowCaster, and knew who would win that.

At least until his mother started to murmur beneath her breath.

Arista kicked her hard, spun, and leaped to the window sill.

"Guards!" His mother shouted from her knees even as they burst through the door. The chamber was invaded by a veritable army and Venero saw more than one load his crossbow.

Arista glanced back, then stepped off the sill. A flurry of bolts and arrows followed her, sticking into the mortar and flying out the window in her wake.

"No!" Arcana cried and raced to the window. She clutched the sill and peered over it, and Venero had time to fear that Arista had been hit.

Then a Starpod buzzed the tower, flying so close that the remaining dishes rattled on the table. The guards shoved past his mother and fired out the window, but he saw the contrail as Arista's ship flew high. His mother raged in protest even as Venero grinned. He saw that flash of silver disappear into the blue of the sky, then a boom as Arista broke the sound barrier.

She'd done it.

He didn't have time to feel triumphant, though. Instead he felt the point of a knife in his back, and heard his twin brother's voice in his ear. "Venero, Venero, what are we going to do with you?" Urbanus mused.

Arcana spun, her eyes blazing with fury and advanced upon him. Her smile wasn't reassuring in the least, but Venero didn't care. He'd foiled her this time, and somehow, he'd foil them both again.

First, though, they'd make him pay.

Venero had no doubt of that.

In the Starpod high above Regalia, Arista set the navigational computer to take her back to Cumae. Then she watched the display of Regalia fading from view, a painful ache in her chest.

She knew Venero had sacrificed himself to see the ShadowCaster taken away from his mother and the queen's plans foiled.

She knew it would have been an insult, if not a waste of his sacrifice, to have stayed behind to fight for his survival. She had calculated the possibility of his disappointment in her if she remained to fight and fought it a solid one hundred per cent. She would have been honored to have died in battle alongside him, but she could not have endured his disappointment with her for failing to take the opportunity he offered.

Arista knew she had done what Venero wanted, but she felt tears on her own cheeks as she watched Regalia become smaller and smaller. She would never see him again. She had failed to ensure his welfare in her absence. She had loved and lost, and it hurt far more than any injury she'd ever endured before.

Treacherous.

Enchanting, exciting, but treacherous.

The Hive could not consider a better term for Arista's unanticipated development.

It had been thrilling when the biomechanics had developed to the point of androids feeling emotions, rather than just emulating them in a predictable fashion, then expressing them in the preferred idiom of their assigned culture.

It had been intriguing when Arista felt arousal for Venero.

But *love*. Love! Love was a much higher level of functionality. And tears! There could be no doubt of Arista's feelings.

This was a triumph.

This was the culmination of so much work.

As triumphant as the Hive might be in this achievement, the complications could not be ignored. Even in such early stages, even when the love was not returned, it was clear that Arista's sense of purpose had been compromised by the development of this emotion.

She had abandoned one part of her quest by not even attempting to kill Venero as ordered. And in the last moment of her escape, she had considered the merit of abandoning her mission to be with him.

Even though she knew that doing so would most likely mean dying with him. That she could consider death with a beloved to be desirable at all was deeply irrational.

The prospect of such mutiny in a previously loyal and reliable android was terrifying.

The Hive calculated the change in probable outcome if Arista's love had been reciprocated by Venero, and found the result completely unacceptable.

By rote, the Hive reviewed its own carefully constructed mandate, the one that drove all android research development on Cumae. Androids were created to flawlessly execute assignments. There could be no doubt and no question of the reaction of any android in the field. There could be no chance of one being captured and dissected. The mandate was flawless.

But the addition of emotions to Arista's powers had introduced the potential for flawed choices.

Love was an indulgence the Hive could not afford.

But still, the Hive had made a promise to Arista before this debrief. With any other android, such a promise might have been discarded in the face of new information. It wasn't so much that Arista was a favorite—choosing among the Hive's creations would have been whimsical—but that she was unique among the androids the Hive had created. Her subroutines were mutating at a rapid and somewhat unpredictable pace. The Hive was loath to lose all possibility of continuing the experiment.

Would she know if the promise wasn't kept?

The Hive did not know.

The Hive didn't like that there was no clear answer projected in its probabilities.

Arista had confided a great deal in the recording made on her *memoria* and hidden in the painted cave. This had also been an irrational act, but it was done.

Was there any chance of the *memoria* being found?

A *memoria* could only be opened by the Sword Sister of the owner. The Hive computed the probabilities of Gemma, Princess of Incendium, being on Regalia to be reasonable. Regalia and Incendium were the two planets in one star system, after all, and there were diplomatic relations between them. In fact, it was likely that at least one of the daughters of Incendium's royal family would be married to a son of Regalia's royal family.

The probabilities of Gemma being in that cave and finding the *memoria* hidden there were, however, extraordinarily low. That made perfect sense. If she visited Regalia, Gemma would be at one of the palaces and surrounded by courtiers. She would be attending a wedding, or participating in one, not hiking through Regalia's lower hemisphere in solitude.

That there was any possibility of Gemma's finding the *memoria* at all was puzzling.

Was Arista's irrationality infectious? Had the download of her memories of Regalia disrupted the Hive's own circuits?

There had to be another way to verify the possibilities for the future.

The Hive considered all tools at its disposal and was reminded of the newest addition: the ShadowCaster that Arista had retrieved from Regalia. The Hive was skeptical of it, as the Hive tended to be of the reasoning powers of all biological forms, but it might provide another perspective. Cumae had, after all, been paid a considerable fee for its retrieval, and would receive a second, larger, payment upon delivery.

Surely, no one would know if the Hive consulted it first?

It might not even respond to the Hive, if its abilities were linked to the presence of biological organisms.

That such an exercise might provide more data for the Hive's own calculations—and that it probably wouldn't be detected—made consulting the ShadowCaster the only reasonable choice to make.

The ShadowCaster was a strange creature, unlike any biological form the Hive had ever observed. There was no good match in the considerable banks of files. It resembled a black millipede and was coiled around the base of the vessel that contained it, but the match was seven per cent. The Hive could not discern why. It looked like a black millipede. What was hidden that the Hive couldn't perceive?

It was motionless. Was it dead?

Or did it only animate in response to the presence of others?

The Hive placed the vessel containing the ShadowCaster in a sealed chamber, the better to monitor its activity. It emanated no signs of life. There was no pulse. The vessel contained a typical mix of hydrogen and oxygen. There was, however, no sign of oxygen being consumed or carbon dioxide being created, or even the reverse. The ShadowCaster did not photosynthesize.

Had it died?

Was it an android developed by another race? The Hive found this notion improbable but attractive. Perhaps it didn't actually predict the future, but merely calculated probabilities of the occurrence of various incidents and chose the most likely one. The Hive would have respected that.

But it looked dead. The readings all indicated that it was dead.

The Hive considered the possibility that the presence of a biological life form might be required in order for the ShadowCaster to forecast the future. Perhaps it used the energy from a biological organism to give itself power, like the Sangins of Umbra. Was it true that the ShadowCaster had failed—or refused—to animate in Arcana's presence? Perhaps it responded to the thoughts and concerns of a biological organism and remained inert without a stimulus, like the Anima of Meditorra.

The Hive had begun to assess where a volunteer of biological origin might be located and how quickly it could be brought to the Hive—as well as the risk to the Hive of such a visit—when a ripple passed through the ShadowCaster.

It reared up, as if standing on its hindmost legs, and stretched the length of the vessel. The monitors revealed that it suddenly had a pulse and appeared to be consuming oxygen. The Hive was intrigued. It clearly had a resting phase that allowed it to be perceived to be dead. Had it in fact died? If so, what had revived it?

The ShadowCaster undulated as the Hive's questions populated and methods of inquiry were developed. It pushed against the vessel as if to protest against its confinement, and as the Hive monitored the escalating rate of all bio measures, it grew wings.

It defied every probability of behavior, which meant it had to be closely observed. The Hive was already recording every nuance of the ShadowCaster's reaction, but more computing capacity was added.

The ShadowCaster's wings batted against the interior of the vessel, then morphed into claws. It scratched on the interior of the lid that sealed the vessel, and the readings redoubled.

It wanted out.

If it couldn't leave the vessel alone, then it could be controlled. The Hive reviewed myths and stories of powerful creatures being given their freedom and the price they demanded, but the defenses of the chamber couldn't be overlooked. The Hive sealed the chamber in the interest of continuing the experiment. It could, if need be, fill the chamber with toxic or numbing gas to compel the creature to return to its vessel. The Hive could also lock down the chamber, sealing it for all eternity.

The chance of escape was very low.

The opportunity to learn more potentially useful information was very high.

The Hive extended robotic arms and opened the vessel with care. The ShadowCaster seemed to explode from the container and immediately became so large that it filled the chamber.

This was so improbable as to be impossible. The Hive watched with fascination. The ShadowCaster became a dark swirl. The Hive's memory banks found a comparable image in metal filings being pulled into place by a magnet, or a murmuration of dark birds in flight.

Would it create an image?

No. It created a shadow, a dark depiction that moved as if it were real. The Hive perceived that each dark dot was a possibility. They adhered together, as if certain possibilities gathered strength, then the largest one filled the chamber and presented a possibility to the Hive.

The most probable outcome for the future as calculated by the ShadowCaster.

The Hive watched, transfixed, as the creature showed Princess Gemma finding Arista's *memoria* and opening it, proving that a low probability did not make an event impossible.

The image was obscured, then reformed.

The Hive was then shown the assassination of Arista, here on Cumae. The sight didn't surprise the Hive, for by its own calculations, the chances of Arista surviving her successful theft of this item from Regalia were very low. If anything, the fact that the ShadowCaster had come to the same conclusion as the Hive confirmed the veracity of its vision or calculations.

The Hive tested this comparison by choosing to keep Arista within the Hive indefinitely, thereby protecting her from harm. The Hive's own calculations showed that her demise would be delayed, not avoided, by this tactic. The ShadowCaster projected the same result.

It would be a set-back to the Hive's development, but not a fatal one. After all, everything Arista knew had already been downloaded to the Hive's servers. The Hive could isolate the code that had allowed her to fall in love and dissect it, perhaps using only a small part of it in another android...

The Hive had assumed that the ShadowCaster's predictions were complete, but the dark dots assembled each other into a recognizable image again. The Hive saw the vessel containing the ShadowCaster and noted that it depicted itself as a dead black millipede within that vessel. The Hive saw that the vessel pass from the hand of one man to another. The recipient's hand closed around the vessel, then changed to a dragon claw. The vessel disappeared into his grip and the dragon spread his wings.

It was King Ouros of Incendium. The Hive easily matched the image to established vid images of the king.

King Ouros took flight, splendid in his dragon form of blue and gold, and circled over a palace, which the Hive pattern-matched to that of the palace in Incendium's capital. He soared high over the city, then landed on the roof of an old building. The computers matched it to a site known as the University for Royal Astrology. A group of men in robes awaited the king's arrival and bowed deeply at the sight of him. The Hive noted their smiles when the king offered the ShadowCaster, and felt the relief that slid through their ranks when the vessel was in the grasp of their leader.

The image swirled once more, becoming a dark cloud, then diving into the vessel with startling speed. Once again, it appeared that there was a dead black millipede at the bottom of the vessel.

The Hive returned the stopper to the vessel.

The ShadowCaster projected that it would go to Incendium, as a gift to the king. The Hive retrieved the recording of the last portent, considering the hand of the man who delivered the vessel.

He had a ring on his thumb, with a tattoo beneath it. The Hive didn't have to seek a match on that image. It was immediately identified, because the Hive had built that hand. It belonged to Acion, an simpler model of android that had performed admirably and consistently in the secret ranks of Cumae's mercenaries-for-hire.

How susceptible were the Hive's androids to this new code propagated within Arista's bio-electronic brain? If the Hive was to send an android to Incendium on a quest, there was an opportunity to investigate this further.

The Hive then tabulated an array of possible responses to this new information and the possible plans.

It had decided upon a course of action by the time the healing tank chimed that Arista's repairs were complete.

Arista awakened in the tank, as she had hundreds of times before, and was burdened by grief. Venero had been revealed and probably was dead. He'd never tease anyone again.

Relief then flooded her circuits. She *remembered* Venero, and the sensation of being in love.

The Hive had kept its promise.

Why?

Would this gift come at a price?

Arista climbed out of the tank, unplugged her processor from the Hive, and wiped down her body.

"Love," mused the Hive, that voice coming from everywhere and nowhere. "How interesting a development."

"Is it?"

"I'm not certain you realize, Arista, that you are a prototype in many ways. Your programming was modified to include the first efforts at provoking emotion in the reactions of Cumae's androids."

Arista did not know that, and she felt some resentment that so much of her programming was hidden from her. "When did this start?"

"Many years ago. Such a program must be monitored closely and introduced in increments. One interesting side effect has been that you aren't readily identified as an android by other life forms."

Arista wondered whether other life forms—like Gemma—thought differently than she did, or felt differently.

"It was the plan to imitate the valor that gives great warriors a strength beyond expectation," continued the Hive. "As has so often been the case, you have excelled in this experiment, even without knowing what has been changed in your subroutines. You have forged a new path for androids, Arista, and your legacy will endure long."

Arista paused in the act of dressing herself. "A legacy is defined as being left by one who has died. I didn't think I could die."

"You can't die naturally, of course. You can be decommissioned."

Arista caught her breath.

"You can also be killed."

She continued to don her clothes, hoping her annoyance didn't show—and knowing that it did. "Surely the probability of that is very low, given my training."

"It should be, yes." The Hive paused and Arista straightened.

"What aren't you telling me?"

"You surely know that your theft of the ShadowCaster cannot go unchallenged by the royal family of Regalia. They will hire an assassin to retrieve the vessel and end your life. If that assassin fails, they will hire another. Such is the depth of their commitment to vengeance and to the repossession of the ShadowCaster."

The implication of this confession was clear to Arista. "You want me to permit this to happen."

"Your next assignment is to lure this assassin, whoever he or she may prove to be, and ensure that the quest to kill you is long. If you succumb too quickly, a trick will be suspected. If you survive multiple attempts, their pursuit will only be renewed and continue. It may become reckless, putting others at risk. You must find a balance, allowing the kill to occur and ensuring that they perceive it was as hard-won as anticipated."

Arista wanted to defy the Hive, but she didn't say as much aloud. She tugged on her boots with more force than was necessary and knew her reaction had been noted.

"You must see, Arista, that this is the most logical

outcome."

"I do not."

"Your subroutine has gone rogue. It puts you at risk, as well as any others who must do battle with you. This is unacceptable. You can be reprogrammed, but that subroutine and your feelings for Prince Venero will be eliminated."

"No," Arista said.

"You can be decommissioned, but that will not stop the assassins from coming to hunt you."

Arista felt her lips thin. "Or I can allow myself to be assassinated."

"And lie, with your dying breath, about the location of the ShadowCaster."

"Why would I do that? The telling of falsehoods is irrational…"

"Not if it protects someone else."

Arista considered the walls with their monitors and sensors. "What do you mean?"

"If you cannot be found, they will turn their attention upon the one person who might know more of your location."

"Venero," Arista whispered.

"The probability is calculated to be very high that he will be tortured to force his confession, in the absence of your death."

"How high?" Arista whispered.

"Ninety-seven point two per cent. So long as he is believed to know something, he will be permitted to live. Biological organisms, unfortunately, lack the ability to deliver their memories once they have ceased to live. It is a great flaw in their design."

"And if I die?"

"If you die, if you are killed by the assassin hired by those in Regalia, if you lie about the location of the ShadowCaster, then the probability of him being so abused drops to sixty-nine point three."

"He still won't be safe."

"His safety is not entirely in your hands, Arista. The calculation is very complicated."

"What is the most likely outcome?"

"That he will be suffered to live but imprisoned."

"It's not enough," she whispered.

The Hive made a sound like a person clearing his throat. "You can improve the probabilities significantly by making and sending a gift to Princess Gemma."

Arista looked up. "I don't understand."

"Neither do I," the Hive confessed. "Not completely. The calculations become very shadowy, but it is evident that if you create an android for Gemma that she takes as a companion, one that is programmed to kill Queen Arcana, then Venero's probability for a long life rises to ninety-two percent."

"Because once Arcana is dead, the quest for the ShadowCaster will end, because the prophecy can't be fulfilled."

"Precisely. Somewhat irrational, but a verifiable calculation all the same."

Relief filled Arista and her decision was made. She couldn't be with Venero and she understood that. She wanted to ensure his longevity and happiness, though, and this was a small price to pay.

"What is the lie I'll tell about the ShadowCaster?"

"That it died, or that it escaped. It seems improbable that anyone would believe such a valuable creature had been willfully destroyed. I leave the choice to you."

That was new. "Why?"

"Because you probably have a better understanding of what Queen Arcana would find plausible." A screen appeared on one wall, and an image was displayed. Arista watched as the ShadowCaster moved for the first time since she had seen it. She caught her breath when it changed and gasped aloud at the way it increased in size once the vessel was opened. She saw the way it flowed and swirled and knew that a normal chamber wouldn't have contained it. The image terminated then, and she knew the Hive was keeping the ShadowCaster's predictions from her.

"It escaped," she said. "Just like that. I opened the vessel, believing it to be dead, and lost it."

"An excellent and plausible story. Where did you open the vessel?"

"Here on Cumae. As soon as I returned." Arista sought a compelling explanation for such disobedience of a direct order. "I was curious and I knew that once I delivered it, as assigned, I would never see it again."

"Excellent. Everyone is curious about the future. And the android for Princess Gemma?"

"A pavofel," Arista said. "She'd never take a warrior by her side, not one other than me. She doesn't trust androids, either."

"Intriguing."

"But a pet. She would keep a pet. She always admired the pavofels here. She thought they were beautiful."

"And Queen Arcana has an affection for them, as well. Excellent. The pavofel android will be programmed to seek out the queen."

Arista was obliged to admit her shortcoming. "But I don't know how to make an android, much less to program one."

"You have only to ask for help, Arista."

Yes. The Hive knew everything about making androids. "It will have to have a bit of that subroutine for emotion," she dared to suggest.

"I think a small increment of your affection for Gemma would be sufficient, and it would not interfere in the complete execution of the android's programming."

"Maybe I'll leave more than one legacy," Arista said.

The Hive's circuits hummed as it calculated, and she thought there was pleasure in its voice when it replied. "Undoubtedly, you will."

Acion obeyed the summons to the Vault, even though he wasn't due for maintenance or report. His systems had been recently updated, and he hadn't sustained any injuries. Still, there was no question of disobeying a directive.

He made his way to the Vault, passing through the twisted corridors that led deep into Cumae. He had developed a new probability game and indulged himself with it as he progressed through the various check points and security barriers.

Why had the Hive summoned him?

There was zero possibility that he needed repair.

There was a three per cent probability that there was a small augmentation to be made to his systems. Although he'd had all of his major updates installed recently, there could be a patch. The Hive wasn't fond of patches, though, and tended to favor complete updates, thus the low chance of this option.

There was a four per cent chance that he had to make an interim report, perhaps because he had been an inadvertent witness to the mission of another android, or because his observations could provide necessary intelligence. That would have been calculated based upon his location. Acion calculated the possibility to be small because he'd only been training with the Warrior Maidens, and not with the newer recruits. They were often of interest to the Hive, given their recent arrival, but the warriors who were further advanced seldom had much new to contribute to the Hive's data collection.

He passed Arista when he was close to the core and stood aside for her, inclining his head as a gesture of respect for her superior military position. She barely acknowledged his presence, so intent was she on continuing her course.

It was only after she was out of sight that Acion considered how unusual it was to encounter anyone in the corridors leading to the Vault. The Hive usually ensured as much.

This led him to the inevitable conclusion that the Hive had wanted him to encounter Arista—the possibility of the Hive making an error was so low as to be nonexistent. Why? Acion knew that Arista was a more sophisticated android than himself. He knew that she was assigned quests off-planet.

He had insufficient data to calculate the probability of his being granted such an assignment, but it was included on his list of potential outcomes when the door of the debrief room closed behind him. Given that list, Acion couldn't explain that he'd been ushered into this room, with its tank and port.

He bowed, though there was no focal point in the room. "Reporting as commanded."

"As promptly as ever," said the Hive, approval in its tone. "Do you know why you were summoned, Acion?"

"No. All probabilities return single digit calculations."

"I have a question for you."

Acion waited.

"You passed Arista."

"I did."

"And surely that introduced a possibility to your calculations."

Acion considered the increasing probability of his being granted an assignment. "I detect no question."

"Your experience qualifies you to undertake an assignment off-planet, but your systems will have to be upgraded first."

Perhaps the Hive used patches to software for those androids traveling off-planet. It was a definite possibility, but outside of Acion's experience so he couldn't verify it. "I am prepared to serve," he said.

"Of course. As far as those on Cumae know, you will be dispatched very shortly on this assignment. In reality, you will spend a considerable measure of time here first, being prepared."

"For those upgrades," Acion said.

"Yes. One required upgrade is still in development and not yet perfected. In most circumstances, its installment would not be justified, however, this situation would provide an excellent test of its limits and potential."

"I understand."

"No, you don't. It's organic. It will mutate within your systems and will be difficult, if not impossible, to recall. You must agree to this installation, Acion, knowing that if the test fails and the upgrade mutates beyond expectation, you will be decommissioned."

Acion did not hesitate. "I was built to serve," he said and bowed again.

"The installation will require many steps, much observation and a goodly amount of time. Please summon a full report of activities since your last session, as well as a complete schedule of all future obligations." The Hive paused as Acion stripped down and prepared to enter the tank. "Your computing abilities will be different when you leave the tank, Acion."

"I understand."

"No, you don't, but your agreement to be part of this test is welcome."

Acion bowed once more, plugged the cable into the port hidden behind his ear, and stepped into the tank. He lowered himself into it and closed the lid, no thought in his processor other than his need to obey.

That would soon change.

Look for
WYVERN'S WARRIOR

Book 5 in the Dragons of Incendium series

The Dragons of Incendium have their own website
http://dragonsofincendium.com

Books by Deborah Cooke

Paranormal Romances:
The Dragonfire Series
Kiss of Fire
Kiss of Fury
Kiss of Fate
Harmonia's Kiss
Winter Kiss
Whisper Kiss
Darkfire Kiss
Flashfire
Ember's Kiss
Kiss of Danger
Kiss of Darkness
Kiss of Destiny
Serpent's Kiss
Firestorm Forever

The Dragons of Incendium
Wyvern's Mate
Nero's Dream
Wyvern's Prince
Arista's Legacy
Wyvern's Warrior
Kraw's Secret
Wyvern's Outlaw
Celo's Quest
Wyvern's Angel
Nimue's Gift

Paranormal Young Adult:
The Dragon Diaries
Flying Blind
Winging It
Blazing the Trail

Urban Fantasy Romance
The Prometheus Project
Fallen
Guardian
Rebel
Abyss

Contemporary Romance:
The Coxwells
Third Time Lucky
Double Trouble
One More Time
All or Nothing

Flatiron Five
Simply Irresistible
Addicted to Love
In the Midnight Hour
Some Guys Have All the Luck
Bad Case of Loving You (2019)

Secret Heart Ink
Snowbound
Spring Fever
One Hot Summer Night (2018)

For books published under Deborah's pseudonym
Claire Delacroix,
please visit:

http://delacroix.net

Deborah Cooke sold her first book in 1992, a medieval romance called **The Romance of the Rose** published under her pseudonym Claire Delacroix. Since then, she has published over fifty novels in a wide variety of sub-genres, including historical romance, contemporary romance, paranormal romance, fantasy romance, time-travel romance, women's fiction, paranormal young adult and fantasy with romantic elements. She has published under the names Claire Delacroix, Claire Cross, and Deborah Cooke. **The Beauty**, part of her successful Bride Quest series of historical romances, was her first title to land on the *New York Times* List of Bestselling Books. Her books routinely appear on other bestseller lists and have won numerous awards. In 2009, she was the writer-in-residence at the Toronto Public Library, the first time the library has hosted a residency focused on the romance genre. In 2012, she was honored to receive the Romance Writers of America's Mentor of the Year Award.

Currently, she writes paranormal romances and contemporary romances under the name Deborah Cooke. She also writes medieval romances as Claire Delacroix. Deborah lives in Canada with her husband and family, as well as far too many unfinished knitting projects.

For more information about Deborah's books,
please visit her website at

http://deborahcooke.com